ANN TURNBULL grew up in south-east London but now lives in Shropshire. She has always loved reading and knew from the age of ten that she wanted to be an author. Her numerous books for children include *Alice in Love and War*, *A Long Way Home* and *House of Ghosts*, as well as her Quaker trilogy – *No Shame, No Fear* (shortlisted for the Guardian Children's Book Award and Whitbread Award), *Forged in the Fire* and *Seeking Eden*. For younger children, she has also written *Greek Myths*, illustrated by Sarah Young.

Local history was the inspiration behind the powerful and poignant trilogy of books about a mining family, the Dyers. *Pigeon Summer*, *No Friend of Mine* and *Room for a Stranger* follow the family and its fortunes from 1930 through to the early years of the Second World War. *Pigeon Summer* has been dramatized for TV and radio as well as being shortlisted for the Smarties Book Prize and the WH Smith Mind Boggling Books Award.

Find out more about Ann Turnbull and her books at **annturnbull.com**

Praise for *No Friend of Mine*

"A masterly book." *School Librarian*

"A brilliant book which should be at the top of every 9- to 12-year-old's reading list." Sunday Telegraph

"Turnbull examines the class conflict from both sides, rigorously but without preaching. The material differences between the boys are picked out in revealing details." Geraldine Brennan, *TES*

"A thought-provoking and realistic read."
School Library Journal, US

"This fine historical novel evokes the time and place with spare detail. The class conflict is a burning reality ... just as strong is the personal struggle with friends and enemies."
Hazel Rochman, *Booklist, US*

"[Turnbull] has a clear and lively style... [The] perennially relevant themes of relations between the haves and have-nots and the difficulties of flawed friendship make it appealing to fans of contemporary dramas as well as historical fiction."
Bulletin of the Center for Children's Books, US

No Friend of Mine

ANN TURNBULL

**WALKER
BOOKS**

First published 1994 by Walker Books Ltd
87 Vauxhall Walk, London SE11 5HJ

This edition published 2014

Text © 1994 Ann Turnbull
Cover photograph © Bert Hardy / Gettyimages

Acknowledgement: The two lines of poetry quoted on page 10 are from
"The Wild Swans at Coole" by W.B. Yeats

The right of Ann Turnbull of to be identified as author of this
work has been asserted by her in accordance with the
Copyright, Designs and Patents Act 1988

This book has been typeset in ITC Caslon

Printed and bound in Great Britain by Clays Ltd, St Ives plc

British Library Cataloguing in Publication Data:
a catalogue record for this book is available from the British Library

ISBN 978-1-4063-2477-8

www.walker.co.uk

To Sally Christie

Chapter One

Lennie knew they would be waiting for him. As he came out through the school gates he saw them, on the corner by the King's Arms: Reggie Dean, Alan Revell, Bert Haines.

Every day for nearly half a term they had caught him there. If he left school early they sprinted after him. If he hung back, they waited; they never tired of waiting.

Not today, Lennie decided. He'd had enough. He had to try and give them the slip.

He eased himself out of the gateway alongside a crowd of girls, turned left instead of right, then pelted down the road and round the corner into Waters Lane.

Halfway down the lane, where a footpath led into the woods, he stopped for breath. He glanced round – and saw them coming, dodging between groups of dawdlers.

In panic he plunged onto the woodland path and down into the dingle. At the bottom was a shallow brook forded by stones. He sprang from stone to stone, hearing behind him the familiar voices: "Hey! Dyer!" "Miss Neale's pet!" He turned to see them charging down the slope.

He wouldn't run. He wouldn't give them the satisfaction. He stood on the far bank and faced them.

Bert straddled the ford. "Forgotten the way home, Dyer?"

Alan and Reggie sniggered.

"You're not allowed to play in the water, are you, Mummy's boy?" And, as he spoke, Bert stamped in the stream, sending a spray of water up Lennie's leg.

Bert was the one Lennie was most afraid of. Reggie had been all right last year, until Miss Neale came, and Alan was the sort that would follow any idiot. But Bert was big, with a bashed-in nose and flat, hard eyes. Lennie hated him.

He brushed the water from his trousers and tried

to walk past. Bert shoved him and he staggered and fell into the muddy brook, dropping his coat. His lunch tin clanged on the stepping stones. Reggie kicked it. The lid flew off and an apple core rolled into the water.

Two girls approaching the brook from the other side stopped and stared. One of them shouted, "Leave him alone, can't you? He's never done you any harm."

Lennie knew the girls. They were in his class. He wished they would go away.

He tried to get up. Bert kicked him and he fell again, grazing his knee on a stone.

"I'm telling Miss Neale," said Margaret Palmer.

"Telling Miss Neale," mimicked Alan in a girly voice, but he sauntered off. The other two followed. Bert chucked a screwed-up piece of paper at Lennie as he went.

"Look at his coat!" exclaimed Sylvia Lee. She pulled it out of the water.

Lennie picked up the paper and smoothed it out. With a shock he recognized his own writing. It was a page torn from his school exercise book – this morning's handwriting practice: the date, Friday

22nd October 1937, followed by some poetry.

The trees are in their autumn beauty,
The woodland paths are dry…

Margaret turned to Sylvia and sucked in her breath. "They've torn a page out of his book."

Lennie felt hot with anxiety. Miss Neale hadn't even marked it yet; she'd be furious.

"I'll tell Miss Neale it wasn't you," said Margaret.

Lennie was alarmed. "No! Don't."

He daren't tell on Bert; it would only make things worse. He'd have to pretend it was an accident.

He became aware of Sylvia, holding his coat.

"I could have got that," he growled.

He didn't want their help. He felt a fool. Some other children had appeared and were staring at his bloodied knee and wet clothes.

He put the paper in his pocket, picked up his tin, and turned for home.

But he didn't want to go home. He'd face a wall of questions, arriving there wet and bleeding, with his coat in such a state. If he waited a bit he might dry out and could brush himself down.

He turned off the road and made his way across field paths to Love Lane, on the far side of town, near the brickworks.

There were no other children here. A few cottages were clustered at the top of the lane, but soon the path dwindled to a dirt track that led into woodland. Lennie followed it for half a mile or so. The ground was soft under his feet and in the breeze a scatter of leaves fell continuously: red-gold, amber, yellow, brown. He picked up a crimson cherry leaf. Miss Neale would like that. She had made an arrangement of autumn leaves, nuts, tree bark and toadstools on a table in the classroom. The boys sneered, but Lennie secretly enjoyed it. He imagined his leaf on the table, part of the display. But he wouldn't give it to her. He didn't want her attention; he had too much already. He threw the leaf away.

He saw some big stones scattered around, and went to investigate. They were the remains of a cottage, almost buried in undergrowth. Doors, windows and roof were gone, but parts of the four walls still stood, grey-white amongst the dark holly and elder.

Lennie pulled away the ivy that grew across the doorway, and went in.

It was tiny – a labourer's cottage with an earth floor. The home, perhaps, of someone who'd worked on the land, or at the brickworks, years ago. There were traces of a campfire in the centre: ash and blackened sticks in a ring of stones. But nothing recent. No one had been here for a long time.

This could be my secret place, Lennie thought.

No one would find him here. He could bring sacking to sit on; he could bring some of his things from behind the settee.

Lennie had no space of his own at home. Behind the settee he kept a few sheets of paper – opened-out envelopes and sugar bags – with his conkers and marbles, some comics, a dried flattened frog and a jay's feather. Every so often when Mum was cleaning she would move the settee, and if she wasn't in a good mood his treasures were in danger of being thrown away.

But here – here he could bring a tin, then even his paper would keep dry. And a mug. And matches. He could light a fire, boil water, make tea, even roast things… Lennie had never caught an animal in his life, let alone cooked it on a campfire, but he'd watched enough Tarzan films to know how it should be done.

The thought of cooking reminded him that he was hungry. It must be tea time. Phyl and Mary would be home from work and Mum would be laying the table.

He gave a last look round the cottage.

I'll come back tomorrow, he thought, first thing. And next week – next week was half term, a whole week without school.

The mud drying on his clothes no longer seemed important as he ran home.

Chapter Two

Lennie went in through the back garden gate, past the pigeon loft. A steady cooing came from inside. Overhead a flock was circling: the hen birds, out for their exercise. That meant Mary was home.

He brushed at his clothes as he walked up the path. Most of the mud seemed to have dropped off.

Inside, Doreen was kneeling on the mat by the fire, reading *The Girl's Own Paper*. Mum was getting the cutlery out of the dresser drawer.

Doreen said, "Lennie's bleeding, Mum."

Lennie glared at her.

Mum turned round. "Oh, Lennie, what have you been doing?"

"I fell."

"Again? Where have you been? It's late; the girls are home from work. Oh, and there's mud all down you! Look at the state of your coat."

"I dropped it."

"Why don't you *wear* it? It's cold now. You've got to look after yourself, with your chest."

"It's not cold. The others never wear coats."

"You don't want to get ill again."

Lennie could only dimly remember the time when he had been so ill that his mother was afraid he would die. He'd had whooping cough, followed by pneumonia. He was five then; now he was eleven.

"I'm all *right*," he said.

"It's those boys," said Doreen. "Picking on him."

Mum looked at him. "Do they, Lennie?"

"Sometimes." Lennie frowned at the lino.

"You'll have to stand up to them, you know."

"I do."

He wanted to get away. He didn't want this. Bert and the others were his problem; private. None of Doreen's business.

He was relieved when he heard footsteps on the stairs.

Mary had changed out of her work clothes, but her hair was still pale with clay dust, and Lennie could see the dust ingrained in the creases in her shoes and in her hands. She worked in the press shop at the tile works.

"Hiya, kid." She smiled at Lennie.

"Look at the state of him," said Mum, turning to Mary for support.

But Mary wasn't interested in Lennie's state. She said, "I'm starving. What's for dinner?"

"Potato pie with a bit of bacon." Mum sounded apologetic. "I'll go shopping tonight."

Friday was payday. Lennie hoped they might have fish and chips tomorrow.

Phyl came downstairs with her hair in curlers.

"Come on, Phyl," said Mum, "let's get this table laid. Lennie, pop down the road and fetch your dad from Bob Wright's. Those two, they forget all about food when they're talking politics."

Lennie went out and ran down the arched passageway between the houses and into the street. Dad was already coming out of Bob Wright's, with a bundle of papers under one arm. He made his way slowly towards Lennie, then stopped by Mrs

Richards' gate, and leaned on it, wheezing.

Lennie came up. "You all right, Dad?"

"Just getting my breath." He moved on.

Dad had been off work for a month and wasn't getting better. Lennie slowed his pace to match as they went down the passage and into the house.

Mum took Dad's coat and hung it up. "You should have stayed in."

"Got to move – can't sit about," Dad retorted.

He dumped the pile of papers on the dresser. They were ideas for a leaflet the two men had been discussing. The Union was campaigning to get pithead baths installed at Old Hall Pit.

"Springhill's got them, and Staveley, and all the deep mines up Stafford way. They've got to give in," Dad said as they ate.

"It's such a small pit," said Mary. "They won't want to be bothered."

"They're bothered enough to make money out of the coal."

"Oh, I'm not arguing with you. I'm all for it."

"It's Wildings that own Old Hall, isn't it?" said Mum. "Tight, they are."

"All bosses are tight," said Mary. "There's a

rumour going round Lang's that they're going to cut wages. We'll not stand for that."

Mary was only nineteen, but already she was active in the Union.

"If they're wanting to cut wages they'll never agree to your equal pay nonsense," said Phyl.

That set Mary off, as Lennie had known it would.

Equal pay for women was a thing she'd campaigned for ever since starting at the tile works.

He didn't join in the conversation but privately he championed Mary. She was his favourite sister: big, brave, confident – all the things he wasn't.

Phyl soon lost interest in the argument. "Oh, don't lecture me, Mary," she laughed. "I'm going out. Got to get ready."

She darted upstairs, and came down wearing lipstick, with her hair brushed out in waves.

"What are you seeing tonight?" Mum asked.

"*Top Hat*," said Phyl. She twirled cautiously in the small space between table and sink. "Fred Astaire and Ginger Rogers."

Mum looked envious. "We ought to go, Tom."

But Dad pulled a face; he didn't like musical comedies.

There was a knock at the back door.

"There's Jim," said Mum. "Off you go, Phyl. Have a good time."

The door closed behind Phyl.

Lennie, about to slip away too, found Dad's attention on him.

"Well, Lennie, how's school?"

"All right."

"Miss Neale pleased with you?"

"She likes my drawings."

"Oh." Lennie could tell Dad wasn't interested in drawings. No one they knew made a living by drawing.

"She says I could get a job in a drawing office. In Birmingham, she says."

"As long as you keep out of that pit," said Mum.

Dad agreed, but Lennie knew it was for different reasons. Mum was worried about Lennie's health – the coal dust on his lungs – but Dad wanted him to get on, get a well-paid job.

Lennie didn't think much about jobs; few people did in Culverton. Boys went down the mine, girls went to the tile or china works – or served in a shop, like Phyl.

Dad had begun wheezing again. Lennie seized his opportunity and fled to the front room.

"Don't go making a mess in there," Mum called.

Doreen followed him in.

"Want to play Ludo?"

"No."

"Snakes and Ladders?"

Lennie liked playing with Doreen, but tonight he had decided to punish her for telling Mum about the gang.

"I'm busy," he said, rummaging behind the settee for his things. "Go away."

Doreen sat on the floor and picked up a red-and-white swirled marble, turning it in the light. "I've got no one to play with."

"Go and play with Rosie Lloyd."

"I don't like her. She smells of wee."

"That's rude."

"It's true. Anyway, she never understands things properly."

Lennie knew what Doreen meant; Rosie was slow-witted, couldn't be much fun to play with.

But he hadn't time for Doreen now. He was thinking about the ruined cottage, how he'd go there tomorrow, what he'd need. Matches were important; he must have a fire. And the tin mug that Dad used to take to work; no one would miss that...

Chapter Three

Someone was there.

He knew as soon as he entered the cottage, even before he saw the jersey – dark blue, unfamiliar – lying on the broken wall.

He felt wary, like a cat trespassing on another's territory. He glanced around. Someone had rearranged the stones of the hearth and dropped a cigarette stub nearby.

He turned back to the door – and found the entrance blocked.

A boy: taller and bigger than Lennie, but about the same age. He had dark hair, and although he was pale-skinned it was not the frail undernourished pallor of some of the children at Lennie's school. There was something different about him. Lennie couldn't think what it was. He looked ordinary enough, and yet. Was it his stance, his expression? Confidence. As if he belonged here and Lennie didn't.

He came in, and Lennie stepped back.

"This is my hide-out," the boy said.

Not aggressively. A statement of fact. His accent was strange: posh.

And that was what was different about his clothes, Lennie realized. They were plain but there were no darns or patches. They fitted, too, as if they had been bought for him.

"I found this place," said Lennie. "I found it yesterday."

"I found it last summer."

Lennie thought of the piled dead leaves, the ashes in the hearth. "You haven't been back, though, not for a long time."

"I've been at school."

The boy spoke as if this were an obvious reason for his not having been back. It wasn't obvious to Lennie. He'd been at school too.

The boy shrugged. "It doesn't matter. No one owns it, do they?"

Lennie felt a surge of relief; he'd been tensing for a confrontation. And he knew he wouldn't have won. Not just because this boy was bigger, but because of the way he talked, because of everything about him.

"I brought my stuff," Lennie said, setting down a battered tin and Dad's enamel mug.

The boy squatted next to him. "What's in the tin?"

"Oh – just things."

The tin contained marbles, conkers, matches and a pencil, but on top of these Lennie had laid his bits of paper, some with drawings on them.

"Let's see," the boy urged.

Reluctantly Lennie took off the lid. He tried to push the drawings aside, but the boy seized them.

"Did you do these?"

"Yes."

"Awfully good. Especially the bird."

Lennie felt pleased. The drawing was of one of Dad's pigeons, Speedwell. He'd sketched her when he was in the loft with Mary. Speedwell was preening, one wing extended, the long feathers fanned out. He had drawn her quickly, catching the essence of her form.

"My dad races pigeons," he said. "I draw them a lot."

"Is your father a miner?"

"Yes. But he doesn't work underground any more. He's got the dust."

"The dust?"

"You know. The coal dust. It's in his lungs. He wheezes all the time."

"Oh. Where do you live?"

"Forty-seven Lion Street."

"What's your name?"

This felt like an interrogation. Why couldn't *he* ask a question?

"Lennie Dyer." He added quickly, "What's yours?"

"Ralph Wilding. I live back there." He gestured towards the other side of the woods.

Lennie understood. "Above the dale? The gentry houses?"

Ralph half smiled. Lennie was not sure whether he was amused or embarrassed by the description.

He wondered why a boy from those big houses would need a den. No, not a den. What had Ralph called it? A hide-out. Lennie liked that word. It sounded as if they were in danger, like outlaws.

Perhaps he was, in a way. But not Ralph – surely no one bullied Ralph?

"What do you do here?" asked Ralph.

"I haven't done anything yet. I thought I could light a fire, and … and that…"

It was hard to explain what he wanted to do.

At the cinema he had seen films about cowboys and Indians. Lennie liked the Indians best; he liked the way they blended into the forest, the way they moved without sound, the signs and secret calls they made. He wanted to be an Indian.

"Look," said Ralph.

A squirrel had darted into view on a nearby tree. It ran down the trunk, stopped, feet splayed, and launched itself lightly to land on the broken cottage wall. Ralph and Lennie both became still. The squirrel flicked its tail up and over in a tense curl, then sprang away again, up into the tree, leaping from branch to branch, and disappearing among the leaves.

Lennie said, "The boys at school throw stones at them."

"That's cruel," said Ralph. "I used to watch them here, last summer. And birds. They come quite close if you keep still."

Lennie scuffed at the hearthstones with his shoe. "Shall we light a fire?"

They went out to search for twigs and branches and came back laden; but the wood they had gathered was damp. They couldn't get it to light, and Lennie had to sacrifice some of his precious paper, which flared up briefly. They threw on holly leaves and were rewarded with a brisk crackle.

"It was easier in the summer," Ralph said. "No one ever came here. I explored all around. I know lots of places in the woods – I can show you, if you like. There's a hollow tree you can get inside, and a mine shaft. I made signs to show the way." He demonstrated, breaking twigs to make an arrow shape.

Lennie said, tentatively, "We could, you know, *be* people... Indians..."

Ralph understood at once. "Yes. Indian braves. We could make up names ... we could make up a code with pictures – a wavy line for water, an exclamation mark for danger..."

Lennie realized the possibilities that sharing the den might bring. You could play better games with two. And Ralph didn't go to the chapel school, so he didn't know that Lennie got picked on and was never chosen for teams. Lennie could start again with him and be a different person, the sort of person he felt like inside.

Ralph said, "Look: you stay here and I'll go and lay a trail. I'll call when it's done – " he made an owl-like sound – "and then you must come and find me. Agreed?"

"OK."

Ralph disappeared into the woods, more noisily than a real Indian brave would have done, but after a while there was silence.

Lennie took out a piece of paper and drew a picture of Indians creeping through a forest. It wasn't very good. He scribbled it out. Instead he began to make up codes as Ralph had suggested. An apple meant "food"; a teepee meant you were "home" – he liked that.

There was no sound from Ralph. Lennie began to think it might all be a trick. Ralph was hiding; or he had gone home; or, perhaps, when he did call, he'd lie in wait and ambush Lennie and make him feel a fool.

Then he heard the call, an unconvincing day-time owl. He put down the paper and pencil and went off in the direction he had heard Ralph take, alert not only for signs but for shaking undergrowth and muffled laughter.

He found the first pointer, a stick arrow. Then a pile of pebbles, then a leaf with a thorn stuck through it, and a log with a newly gouged-out area of soft yellow wood. Further on, a stick arrow led him into brambles that scratched his knees. He blundered about, snapping more twigs than an Indian would have snapped in a lifetime. He couldn't find anything. The unlikely owl-call came again, luring him further in.

He found three sticks freshly broken lying at the bottom of a tree. They didn't seem to point anywhere. He looked up, and saw a foot in a black shoe and navy-blue sock.

Ralph dropped down.

"That sign collapsed," he apologized. "It was meant to be pointing up the tree." Then he added approvingly, "You were quick."

Lennie felt great relief: Ralph wasn't going to play tricks on him.

They walked back to the ruined cottage and threw more branches on the fire. Lennie showed

Ralph his ideas for a picture code and they worked on it together.

Ralph fished in his pocket and drew out a tobacco tin. Inside were three cigarettes. He offered the tin to Lennie, who hesitated, taken aback.

"Don't you smoke?"

"Yes, of course," Lennie said hastily, although the couple of times he'd tried it he'd felt sick and couldn't imagine why adults chose to do it. "Yes … it's just … I mean, we usually collect stubs, you know, that people leave." He looked at Ralph with awe. Three cigarettes. Three whole brand-new ones. "Did you buy them?"

Ralph laughed. "No. I acquired them." He lit one, inhaled, blew out a smooth stream of smoke, and passed the cigarette to Lennie.

Lennie inhaled tentatively and felt himself turning paler. He tried not to cough. Ralph continued: "Susan, my sister, when she's at home, she'll get me to post letters or whatever, and pay me with a ciggy. And sometimes–" he grinned – "I find the odd one or two."

The autumn chill had begun to penetrate Lennie's thin jumper. "Let's move," he said.

They left the fire to die out and went exploring.

Ralph showed Lennie an old mine shaft, uncapped, but clogged with earth and leaves. They jumped on the leaves, tempting danger; imagined falling in, discussed how long you could survive. Lennie found a chance to show off with his stories of mining disasters.

They came to the top of the steep hillside above the dale, and Ralph pointed out the chimneys and gables of his house – solid, red brick, with fancy twisted chimney-pots – rising from the trees below them.

Lennie caught a glimpse of smooth lawn, and a net. "You've got a tennis court," he said.

"Oh, yes," said Ralph. "Susan's mad on tennis. Croquet, too."

Lennie didn't know what croquet was, but he nodded as if he did.

In the afternoon they parted, promising to bring things – marbles, cigarette cards – tomorrow. Lennie ran home happy. Ralph was his friend. He was a bit strange, and he talked funny, but he understood the sort of games that Lennie liked. The boys at school didn't seem to matter any more, and in any case the whole half-term holiday was still to come.

Chapter Four

Lennie propped a row of cigarette cards against the wall of the cottage.

"You go first," he said.

Ralph flicked his card at the row, trying to knock one down. He got one of Lennie's: a film star – Gary Cooper. Lennie tried, and missed. But it didn't matter. He'd won some already. And Ralph had missed on several turns. They were more or less equal. He was glad Ralph wasn't completely superior like the boys at school.

"I'm collecting film stars," said Ralph. "I've got lots of sets: cars, aviators, kings and queens. Oh – and birds. You can have that one if you like. I'll bring it tomorrow. There's an eagle, and gulls and things."

They stayed in the cottage for a while, sharing a cigarette and swapping cards and marbles.

"Can you come back this afternoon?" Lennie asked.

Yesterday, Sunday, they had only met for an hour or so in the middle of the day. Ralph had to go to church on Sunday mornings. Lennie no longer went to chapel with Mum and Doreen, but every Sunday afternoon the whole family went to Aunty Elsie's for tea.

Today Ralph said, "I can stay all day. They won't miss me till dinner time."

"It must be nearly dinner time now," said Lennie. He'd only had a piece of bread and jam and a drink of water for breakfast.

Ralph looked puzzled. Then, "Oh, you mean lunch," he said. "I brought something." He produced a paper bag containing a large slice of pork pie, a piece of cake and an apple. "Cook supplied me. You can share it if you like."

"I'd better go home for dinner – lunch," said Lennie. "I'll come back, though."

And he did. They explored the woodland, went down to the dale, crossed over and watched the goods trucks on the railway line on the other side, found a badger's sett in the woods. They saw a few children from Lennie's school but no one from his class. Lennie deliberately avoided the field where the boys played football, the riverside paths, the woods down Waters Lane.

It was Tuesday before they encountered Bert Haines.

"Hiya," said Bert. He and Alan were on a bridge over a deep forested gully.

"Hiya," said Lennie, without catching Bert's eye. He knew Ralph was a protection. Bert didn't know who he was, or what to make of him.

Lennie had intended to cross the bridge and go up the other side, but his courage failed him, even with Ralph there.

He muttered to Ralph, "I'll show you the old pit shaft," and led him away, up some rough steps and onto a woodland path.

"Friends of yours?" Ralph asked.

"Not really," said Lennie. He wondered if Ralph had guessed about Bert and Alan.

On the edge of town, where there was an old mine shaft beside the road, they met some more boys. One of them was Peter Jones, from Lennie's class. Peter was a quiet sort, not very bright; he'd never bothered Lennie. He was with his brother and some older boys. They had slid under the wires and were throwing stones down the shaft. Lennie and Ralph joined them. The other boys looked at Ralph but didn't question him.

Lennie stared down the shaft. He threw a stone in and listened to the soft far-down plop as it hit water. One of the older boys heaved a brick over the edge. It fell with a satisfying rush, and Lennie saw spray fly up.

"Hey, you lads, away from there!"

The postman, cycling past, was gesturing to them.

Lennie, Peter and Ralph scrambled out. After a moment's silent defiance, the older ones followed.

"Let's go to the canal tunnel," someone said, and they were off, up New Road into the woods at the top and across the Rough. Ralph was asked as they ran, "What's your name?" and "Where do you live?" "The Dale," he answered vaguely to this last, and they were satisfied, though Lennie knew they must have realized that Ralph was "one of the nobs".

Peter, breathing hard as he ran, said, "My cousin saw a ghost in the tunnel."

"He never!"

"He did. It had its head off."

"A man was killed in there. A cart crushed him," one of the older boys confirmed.

"Never had his head off, though, did he?"

"He might have."

"No. If you get crushed it squeezes your chest, like, and breaks your ribs…"

"And there's all blood," added Peter with enthusiasm.

"But it wouldn't take your head off."

"It was a *ghost*," Peter said, as if that explained it.

His brother made ghostly noises and they rolled about, mock fighting. The others joined in.

Lennie grew bored. He tugged at Ralph's sleeve. "Let's go back."

"Can't we see the tunnel?"

"It's nothing. Just an old tunnel. A dead end. Come on."

They ran off.

"You don't know any of these places, do you?" Lennie asked.

"I'm not here much. Only in the holidays. My school's in Gloucestershire."

"Gloucester! That's fifty-seven miles away!"

"Is it?" Ralph looked surprised. "Exactly fifty-seven?"

"Yes. Dad races the pigeons from there."

"They fly there?"

"No, stupid. They fly home. Dad sends them to Gloucester on the train. At the other end they're all released, and then they fly home. Don't you know anything about pigeon racing?"

"Not much," admitted Ralph. "Does your father win?"

"Quite often. He won with Blue Bar this summer. From France, that was. Rennes."

Ralph stopped still. His eyes shone. "Lennie! If I took a pigeon with me when I go back to school on Saturday, it could fly home to you, couldn't it?"

"Yes... If Dad didn't mind. I don't see why he should. It's not too late in the year, although we're not training them now because racing's over till next spring. Shall I ask him?"

"Yes. Please. I'd love to do that."

They passed Bert and Alan on their way back to

the cottage, but this time Lennie walked by without feeling scared of them. He was thinking about Ralph's school, puzzling over it.

"Why do they send you there?" he asked. "All the way to Gloucester?"

"Gloucestershire, not Gloucester. The school's near Cheltenham. It's supposed to be a good school, that's why."

"Supposed to be?"

"Well – I daresay it is."

"Don't you like it, then?"

"It's not too bad. I get by. Do you like yours?"

Lennie shrugged.

Back at the hide-out they shared lunch: Lennie's fish paste sandwiches and Ralph's beef patties – "I persuaded Mrs Martin to give me extra rations for you," Ralph said.

"I like her lemonade," said Lennie.

"Good. I'll tell her."

They spent the rest of the day reading comics and writing each other messages in their secret code. When they parted, Ralph reminded Lennie, "You will ask your father, won't you, about the pigeon?" And Lennie said yes, he would, but he felt a reluctance. After his initial enthusiasm, he had had second thoughts. What would Dad think about him having a friend who went to school in Gloucestershire? A bosses' school?

Chapter Five

Lennie put off asking Dad about the pigeon. Dad was poorly, and bad-tempered because he couldn't get about; he'd hoped to be back at his job in the lamp room at Springhill Pit this week.

I'll ask him tomorrow, Lennie thought. There's plenty of time; it's only Tuesday.

On Wednesday they woke to rain. Lennie stared out at the blurry silhouette of the pithead against the sky, desperate to detect a gleam of blue. How could it rain when he'd planned to go to the hide-out? But the sky was solid grey and the rain battered the window-panes, heavy and relentless.

He decided to ignore it.

"Mum, can I make some sandwiches?" he asked,

rummaging in the larder for the jar of bloater paste.

"You're not going out in this!"

"It'll soon stop."

"Don't be daft. It's set for the day, this is."

"But my friend will be waiting down the woods."

"Surely not? Not in the pouring rain."

Lennie had begun spreading margarine on bread. Mum took the bread away from him and put it back on the larder shelf.

"Mum!" he protested.

"What's got into you, Lennie? I've told you: you're not going out in this – not with your chest."

"I'm not ill!"

Lennie was shouting. When would she ever understand that he wasn't ill?

"You will be if you get soaked through."

There was no arguing with her. He stomped upstairs.

Lennie's favourite place for sulking was the tiny landing between the two bedroom doors. It was dark, and uncomfortable, and no one could see you there because the stairs curved just before the top. But today the space was occupied by Doreen, three dolls and a knitted rabbit. Doreen had chalked sums on a slate and was brandishing a ruler.

"You can't come in my school," she said; then looked up, hopeful: "Unless you're the head-master?"

"You're in the *way*," growled Lennie.

Doreen whacked one of the dolls with the ruler. "Sit up straight, Gladys."

Lennie ran downstairs again and darted to the back door.

"Where are you going?" Mum demanded.

"See the pigeons."

"Well, put your coat on."

"It's only down the garden.

"Put it *on*!"

It was easier to give in. Lennie grabbed his coat from the hook on the door and went out, tossing the coat over his shoulders as he ran down the path to the loft.

The loft was a haven. Dad's hide-out. (Everyone needs a hide-out, Lennie thought.) But Dad wouldn't be there at this time of day.

A contented cooing came from the tiered nest boxes inside. Bright eyes – red, dark brown, dark grey – regarded him with interest but no criticism.

There was some shuffling and fluttering as he moved down the length of the loft, but the birds were used to him and didn't panic. He spoke softly, greeting the ones he knew: Blue Bar, Amelia, Queenie, Boomerang, Speedwell.

Which one could he ask for to lend to Ralph? The more he thought about it the more he felt Dad wouldn't like the idea. After all, Ralph might not take care of the bird properly, he might let other boys get hold of it. And yet. Lennie wanted to have something to show Ralph, something that was important to him.

He went to the door. Surely the rain was lighter now? He willed it to be. Leaving his coat in the loft he slipped out, closed the door carefully, and sprinted through the back gateway and down the lane.

Ralph was there, at the cottage. He'd brought a coat, but it wasn't a droopy gaberdine mac like Lennie's; it was a dark green oilskin, waxed, with a drawstring hood– the sort of thing you saw lifeboatmen wearing in pictures. Ralph had arranged it into a makeshift tent in the most sheltered corner of the cottage.

Lennie squelched across the muddy floor. The soles of his shoes had holes in and his socks felt oozy. He noticed that Ralph was wearing Wellington boots.

"It's still pretty wet in here," said Ralph, as Lennie squeezed in beside him. He smelt of wet wool. "We could go to my house if you like."

Lennie wasn't sure. That big house with the fancy chimney-pots – how could he go in there?

And yet he was curious.

"All right," he said.

Ralph led the way.

"Haven't you got a coat?" he asked. "Or are you too poor?"

Lennie was indignant. "No," he said. "I just forgot it."

Ralph was strange, he thought. None of the Culverton boys wore coats; it was considered unmanly. Not that Ralph was wearing his; he was using it more like an umbrella, and trying to include Lennie under its cover. And Lennie liked the oilskin; he liked its sticky waxed surface and the way the water formed into droplets and rolled off it.

By the time they had slithered down the steep

track to the house, Lennie's shoes felt heavy with mud. He looked at them apprehensively as they approached the red-tiled back doorstep.

"Better leave our shoes in the scullery," said Ralph. He stepped out of his boots just inside the door, and hung up the oilskin.

Lennie took off his shoes and followed Ralph, leaving damp footprints on the tiles. He felt conscious of the holes in his socks.

The scullery led into a huge kitchen with a table in the centre and rows of pots hung on the walls. A woman was mixing pastry at the table while behind her a girl was washing up with a great deal of splashing.

Ralph went in ahead of Lennie, and Lennie saw the woman look up. She had blonde curls and a warm smile.

"I thought you'd soon be back," she said. "Do you want —"

She paused, seeing Lennie.

"I've brought my friend," said Ralph. He introduced them mock formally: "Mrs Martin – Lennie. Lennie – Mrs Martin."

"Hello, Lennie."

The smile was no longer warm. The mouth had tightened, and Lennie sensed hostility behind the greeting. He felt Mrs Martin's quick glance taking in his thinness, his darned jumper, the holes in his socks. She knew he had no right here.

The girl at the sink had stopped splashing and turned round. She was about fourteen, but she stared at Lennie open-mouthed like a small child. Lennie saw that she was simple. He felt a shrinking inside. There was a boy lived near Aunty Elsie who was like that. The other children often jeered at him; Lennie wouldn't do that, but he always kept his distance.

"Stella, dear, don't stare," said Mrs Martin.

She offered hot chocolate and buns, saying to Lennie, as she handed him his plate, "You look as if you could do with building up, Lennie."

The bun was fresh, brown and sticky, lavishly buttered. The hot chocolate filled Lennie with warmth, but Mrs Martin's eyes didn't. He imagined her, this evening, going to Ralph's mother and saying, "I don't know if I ought to mention this, madam, but did you know that Ralph is associating with boys of a common sort…"

If Ralph noticed the atmosphere he didn't show it. He wiped crumbs from his face with the back of his hand, smiled at Mrs Martin and said, "Super. Lennie, come on up to my room."

Reluctant under Mrs Martin's gaze, Lennie followed.

The kitchen led to a passage with tiles patterned in red, blue and brown, and then to blue-carpeted stairs. Lennie's feet sank into softness. He had never seen so much carpet. The stairs were wide and shallow with mahogany banisters, and a broad sweeping curve as different from the twist in the stairs at home as it was possible to imagine. The carpet continued across an expanse of landing surrounded by dark panelled doors. Ralph opened one of the doors and led Lennie into a big airy room overlooking the tennis court and the wooded hillside beyond.

There was lino on the floor, but it was new, not cracked and patched like the lino at home. The room was cluttered with books, pictures, games. Model aeroplanes hung on strings from the ceiling. There was a cricket bat in a corner, there was a stack of boxed games: Ludo, Snakes and Ladders,

Monopoly, Chinese Chequers. And books! A whole shelf of them, all Ralph's. *Robinson Crusoe*, *Tales of King Arthur*, *The Children of the New Forest*, *The Boy's Book of Heroes*...

"Can I look at your books?" Lennie asked.

He liked the King Arthur best, with its detailed drawings of forests and castles, wild boar, horses and falcons.

"You can borrow it if you like," said Ralph.

But Lennie wouldn't dare; it looked too precious.

They spent the morning playing Monopoly. Lennie had never played before, and Ralph won, collecting all the houses, all the rents, all the money. Lennie liked the "chance" cards; they seemed his only hope, but they didn't save him.

At around one o'clock Ralph said, "I'm hungry."

"I didn't bring any food," said Lennie. "Mum wouldn't let me come out."

He described his escape, exaggerating it, making it sound like an adventure.

They went back to the kitchen. As they passed through the hall Ralph picked up a gold cigarette case from the polished table and looked inside. He took a cigarette from the six there and slid it up the sleeve of his jersey. He grinned at Lennie. "Finders keepers."

Mrs Martin gave them slices of pie, apples, and lemonade made with sherbert powder stirred in a jug. Stella ate with them. Lennie was uncomfortable with her, but Ralph talked to her and cracked jokes, making her laugh.

Back in Ralph's room, Lennie said, "That girl – Stella—"

"She's Mrs Martin's daughter. They live in."

"She's mental."

"Does she scare you?"

"Not *scare* exactly…"

"She can't help it."

"Oh, I know. I didn't mean." Lennie felt guilty.

"Look, it's stopped raining," said Ralph. "Come and view the estate."

"What?"

"See the garden, dope. We can play cricket if you like."

Lennie wished they could go back to the woods, but it seemed rude to say so. He followed Ralph down the stairs, and as they reached the bottom the front door opened and a woman came in.

Ralph's mother.

Lennie knew at once that it was her. The grey tweed coat, heavy and expensive-looking; the quick, appraising glance at Lennie. He tensed. She wouldn't want him here; he'd be in trouble now.

But Mrs Wilding merely took off her hat and exclaimed, "Goodness, what a change in the weather!"

She moved towards them, pulling leather gloves from her smooth white hands. "And who's your friend, Ralph?"

None of Mrs Martin's coldness. If she disapproved, she hid it.

"Hello, Lennie," she said. Her smile was like Ralph's.

And it was only as she moved to go upstairs and Ralph and Lennie headed for the scullery, that Lennie, glancing back, saw her catch Ralph's eye and raise her eyebrows.

Chapter Six

"Thought I'd take a look at the birds today," Dad said the next morning. "Check the moult. Start thinking about culling and pairing. Do you want to help, Lennie?"

Lennie didn't know what to say. Mary was the one who usually helped Dad. She'd always been interested; "pigeon-mad", Mum would say. And no doubt as soon as Mary got home this afternoon she'd join Lennie and Dad in the loft. He ought to jump at the chance. But—

"I'm going out," he said. "I promised this friend."

"Who's that, then?"

To Lennie's relief, Dad seemed pleased, not offended; perhaps he had guessed that Lennie didn't often have friends to meet.

"I met him down the woods. His name's Ralph. He doesn't go to our school."

"Oh?" Dad looked up. "C. of., is he?"

Lennie knew Dad was thinking of Victoria Road School, where the churchgoers' children went. He didn't feel able to explain about – where was it? – Cheltenham. Not yet. When he asked for a pigeon he'd have to; and Ralph had reminded him again yesterday; but still he put it off.

"He's clever," said Lennie. "Knows a lot of things, like." He thought of the Latin swear words Ralph had taught him.

Dad seemed pleased. "Well, if you get on together. Some of the lads round here." He shook his head. Dad was clever, read books, studied politics, could out-talk anyone at political meetings. The bosses hated him. "It's education." He began wheezing. "Education's our weapon against the ruling classes, Lennie." He pointed to the stack of leaflets on the dresser. "That little lot'll get old Wilding's back up."

Lennie felt a small shock explode in his mind.

Wilding. George Wilding. The villain. Owner of

Springhill, Old Hall, and several other pits in the area. George Wilding, Unionbasher, stinking rich, with a car, and a big house – and probably fancy chimney-pots and a tennis court too.

It couldn't be. George Wilding was the enemy. He was mean, but Ralph—

He said, aloud, "Ralph's always giving me things. He gave me all his old comics. He gets *The Dandy* and *The Beano*."

"Does he? Lucky lad."

Dad's attention went back to the pigeons. He started talking about last summer's races, and which birds he thought he'd pair up for next season. Lennie half listened. At the back of his mind all the time was the thought: Ralph can't be George Wilding's son. He *can't* be.

His mind brimmed with questions as he ran down Love Lane and into the woods. He had to ask Ralph at once, had to find out if it was true.

But Ralph wasn't there.

Lennie felt foreboding. Ralph had always been the first to arrive. Still, it was early. He gathered sticks for a fire, walked several times out of sight of the cottage and back again, each time hoping to find

Ralph there on his return, each time disappointed.

He decided to light the fire, but the wood was damp and it wouldn't catch. He got out his paper and pencils and tried to invent some more code symbols, but he was too restless. He put them away and paced around the cottage.

It was obvious Ralph wasn't coming. Lennie was sure it was something to do with yesterday. Mrs Wilding must have told Ralph he wasn't to meet Lennie. Or she'd told his father, and George Wilding, who hated miners, had told him to stay in. But would that keep Ralph in? It wouldn't keep *me* in, Lennie thought. He felt slighted.

He looked around the cottage. When he'd first found it, he'd thought of it as a secret place where he could be alone. Now, that idea held no charm for him. He slouched home.

Dad was in the pigeon loft.

"What's up, Lennie?"

"My friend didn't come."

Dad gave him a sympathetic look. "Never mind. Give me a hand with these birds."

Ralph wasn't at the cottage on Friday either. Lennie waited, increasingly hopeless. What could have happened? Perhaps he couldn't get away. But Ralph didn't seem the sort to let anyone stop him. He'd sneak out somehow. Perhaps he simply didn't want to come.

Lennie left the cottage and wandered towards the dale until he was in sight of the chimney-pots of Ralph's house. On an impulse he scrambled down the slope, went in through the back garden gate and up to the back door. In the distance a gardener turned and looked at him.

Lennie knocked on the door. His heart thumped.

Mrs Martin opened the door.

"Oh, Lennie," she said. She didn't smile.

Lennie refused to be intimidated. "Is Ralph in?" he asked.

"Master Ralph," said Mrs Martin, lightly emphasizing the first word, "is spending the day with his father at work; he'll be going into the family business when he has finished his education."

Lennie wasn't interested in Ralph's future, only in today. "When will he be back?"

"He'll be there all day, and tomorrow he's going back to school. You won't be seeing him again, I'm afraid."

The sympathetic words were belied by the satisfaction in her voice. Lennie fumbled for the right thing to say. "Well – tell him – tell him…"

"I'm not a messenger," said Mrs Martin. "You'd better run along now, Lennie. I can't help you."

Lennie turned away. A gulf seemed to have opened between him and Ralph. He heard Mrs Martin shut the door. The gardener was still staring.

I hate these people, Lennie thought; they think I'm nothing.

He ran to the gate and out into the woods. Back at the cottage he kicked the remains of the fire. It was boring without Ralph. He picked up his mug and tin and took them home.

Mum was in the back garden, pegging out washing.

"What's got into you, then?"

"Nothing."

He went indoors, and sat on the stairs reading comics.

Mum came in, cleared the table, and spread a thick cloth on it for ironing. Lennie noticed her hands – red and roughened, with splits around the nails. He remembered Ralph's mother pulling the gloves from her white hands.

I don't belong there, he thought.

"You're a funny one," said Mum. "One minute you can't wait to dash out in the pouring rain, and now it's fine you're mooching indoors." She folded a pillowcase. "You could help your dad with the pigeons."

"I helped yesterday."

The pigeons no longer interested him. Nothing did.

The next morning he woke to the sound of pounding feet overhead and raised voices. Mary and Phyl were arguing again.

He got up, and packed away his bed.

Upstairs a door slammed and footsteps thundered down the stairs. Phyl's voice was a shriek, Mum's – in the kitchen – placating.

"...creased all down the front!" Lennie heard Phyl say. "I laid it that careful on the chair and in she comes and throws her things down anyhow—"

"It'll iron out, Phyl," Mum said.

From upstairs came a bellow from Mary. As Lennie stepped into the kitchen a pair of shoes came flying down accompanied by Mary's voice: "And those, as well. She's taking over the whole room!"

Mum shook her head, and turned to Lennie. "The sooner Phyl's married and out of this place the better. The house is bursting at the seams."

Phyl was at the foot of the stairs now, yelling abuse at her sister. Mary yelled back.

A loud knocking made everyone jump.

Mum clutched at her heart. "Lord, is that the front door? Who'd come knocking at the front door, for heaven's sake?"

The front door was never used, being blocked by a table and a thick curtain to keep out draughts. Everyone used the back door, and nobody knocked. The neighbours called, "Coo-ee!" and the better sort – the doctor or the minister – just walked in.

Lennie ran to the front room window and looked out. On the doorstep stood Ralph. Lennie felt instantly alive again. He banged on the window, pointing towards the passage.

"It's my friend!" he exclaimed, bounding across the kitchen and out of the back door.

He met Ralph halfway down the passage. Their voices rang under the brick arch. Ralph said, "I'm going back to school today. I had to come. I've been with my father—"

"Mrs Martin told me," said Lennie.

"Two whole days at Old Hall, in the offices," said Ralph. "Absolutely dire. I brought you this."

He handed Lennie the King Arthur book.

Lennie stepped back. "I can't!"

"Just to borrow," said Ralph. "It'll only sit in my room till Christmas. Go on."

Lennie took it. He looked around. Should he ask Ralph in? Mum would fuss. She'd show Ralph into the front room. It would be awful.

He gestured to the back garden, where Dad was already pottering in the loft.

"The pigeons?" said Ralph. "Did you ask your father?"

"Not yet," confessed Lennie. He felt a spurt of anger. "Didn't think I'd see you again, did I? You never left a message."

"I couldn't. He took me off so early. Can we ask your father now?"

"All right," said Lennie. "Dad!" he called. "Here's my friend – Ralph."

Chapter Seven

Ralph stepped forward and held out his hand. "Good morning, Mr Dyer."

He's just like an adult, Lennie thought, impressed. Dad, by contrast, seemed unusually awkward. He wiped his hand on his trousers before taking Ralph's.

"Pleased to meet you, Ralph."

"Can Ralph see the pigeons?" Lennie asked.

"Yes. Yes, of course," said Dad.

He led the way into the loft.

Ralph gazed around at the tiers of cooing pigeons.

"I don't suppose you've been in a pigeon loft before, young man?" Dad asked. His voice sounded odd, Lennie thought, falsely jocular; he had never seen his father so ill at ease.

"No, I haven't." Ralph began to ask questions: how far the birds flew, what they ate, what they were called, how the race system worked. Soon Dad had relaxed and began talking animatedly. He let Ralph hold a pigeon, showing him how to contain its fluttering. Lennie was glad he hadn't asked Dad before about lending one to Ralph. He suspected that Dad wouldn't have liked the idea. But now Ralph's enthusiasm would surely win him over.

Ralph had already caught Lennie's eye a couple of times.

"Dad," said Lennie, "Ralph's going back to school this morning, over Cheltenham way. Could he take a pigeon with him and send it back?"

"Cheltenham?" said Dad. He paused; looked at Ralph. Ralph smiled eagerly.

"Oh, no," said Dad. "No, I'm afraid not. These are racing pigeons; worth a bit of money. Can't just send odd ones off on a whim." He frowned at Lennie. "You should know that."

"Just this once," pleaded Lennie. He couldn't explain to Dad how important it felt. "They're not training now. It wouldn't hurt."

"Some haven't finished moulting."

"Only one or two." Lennie was glad he'd helped out in the loft the other day. "There's Blue Cloud. She's in good feather."

Dad sighed. "Well – if you're careful of her, Ralph…"

"Oh, I would be!" exclaimed Ralph. "And I'd send her straight back. I wouldn't let the masters see her. Just the boys in the dorm – a quick look—"

A slight, anxious frown crossed Dad's face.

Ralph added hastily, "Most of the boys won't be there till Sunday night. I'll send her back today. I promise."

"Tomorrow morning," said Dad. "That's a better time. I'll give you some feed for tonight. Give her a drink just before you release her, but no food, mind, else you'll never get rid of her. And no handling. She's not one of my best birds, but if any harm was to come to her…"

"I'll take care," promised Ralph.

Dad moved to the nest boxes. "Get a small basket, Lennie." He caught the blue chequer hen and put her in. Blue Cloud cooed and shifted about.

Lennie and Ralph took the basket and went out to the passage.

"Lennie," said Ralph, "when you get her back you must write and tell me. Tell me what time she arrives."

"And you send a message. Tuck it under her ring."

"Yes! Yes, I will. I'd better go now, before they miss me. I don't want my father to see the pigeon."

"He'll hear it in the car. It'll coo."

"Oh, he won't take me. Cartwright will drive me there – the chauffeur. Cartwright's my friend; he won't say anything. Bye! See you next hols."

He went off, the pigeon basket bumping against his leg.

When Lennie returned to the yard he found Mum and Dad there, talking. Dad was holding the King Arthur book, which Lennie had put down in the loft when he went to fetch the basket.

"Did Ralph give you this?" asked Dad.

"Lent it."

Dad turned the pages reverently. "You'd better take good care of it."

"I don't like him having that," said Mum. "Suppose it got damaged?"

"I'll be careful," said Lennie. "Ralph wanted to lend it to me."

Dad said cautiously, "Ralph seems a nice lad."

"You should have brought him in," said Mum. "I'd have made tea."

"He was in a hurry."

"But it seems rude—"

"Now, Lina, don't fuss," said Dad. He turned to Lennie. "That's a posh-sounding school he goes to in Cheltenham. Boarding school. You'd need money to go there."

"They've got a big house," said Lennie.

"What's his name? Surname, I mean."

Lennie took a breath. "Wilding."

Both parents stared.

Lennie stammered, "I … I think. I mean, it might not be…"

"Wilding's son!"

Lennie's stomach tightened, ready for anger. But Dad let out a gust of laughter, then started to wheeze.

"Oh, Tom, don't get excited," warned Mum.

Dad wheezed some more, laughing still. "And there's me nagging the child to be careful of my pigeon – Wilding's son! I'll say one thing for your friend, Lennie – he's got a lot more charm than his father."

"He's not a bit like his father!" Lennie retorted. "He can't help it if he's George Wilding's son, can he?"

"No, of course he can't," said Mum. "And there's good and bad in everyone. Even you've said, Tom, that Wilding's fair in his dealings."

"Aye, he's fair. What he says he'll do, he'll do. Stickler for the letter. But he's a hard man. Expects everyone to come up to his standards." He laughed, shortly. "I wouldn't like to be his son. His only son. Wilding must take some living up to."

Mum said, "How's he going to feel about Lennie going round there? He's got no time for you, has he?"

Lennie knew Mum was thinking of Dad's Union activities and his claim for compensation for the dust disease. The colliery were denying liability and saying Dad had bronchitis.

"Oh, he wouldn't take it out on the child," Dad assured her.

"But he won't like it…"

She regarded Lennie anxiously.

Lennie felt angry and miserable. He said, "Well, it doesn't matter, any road, because Ralph has gone back to school now and he won't be home till Christmas and that's ages and ages away."

And on Monday, he was thinking, *he'd* be back at school too. And Bert Haines would be waiting for him.

Chapter Eight

"Where did you get these?" Ken Forton demanded. "You never won them, did you?"

The row of cigarette cards propped along the ledge outside the boy's toilets contained unfamiliar cards, not part of the well-known pack that circulated amongst the Culverton boys.

"I did," asserted Lennie. "I won them."

"Who off?"

"My friend."

Lennie became aware that Bert, Alan and Reggie were on the edge of the group listening. He longed to grab his cards quickly, and get away. But he couldn't; that would be cheating. They were in the middle of a game – himself, Ken Forton, Martin Reid and Peter Jones. He had to see it through.

"What friend's that?" asked Ken.

The enemy were standing close to Lennie now – Bert in front, Alan and Reggie a step or two behind. Lennie was reminded of a photo he'd seen in the newspaper the other day. It had been of Oswald Mosley, the British fascists' leader, walking in a London street with two of his followers looming behind him. Bert was like that, Lennie thought. A fascist.

Bert said, "It's that posh twit you were with in the woods last week, isn't it? He's your friend."

"Yes!" crowed Alan. "He was with this posh twit, Ken. We heard him talk,"

"Who's that, then?" Ken asked.

"No one," said Lennie.

"Posh twit was a ghost!" spluttered Alan, laughing and staggering against Reggie.

"Who was it?" Ken persisted. "What's his name?"

"Ralph," muttered Lennie.

"Ralph!" exclaimed Bert in delight. "Walf! Lennie's posh fwend is called Walf!" Cries of "Walf! Walf!" came from Reggie and Alan, degenerating to "Woof! Woof!"

"Leave him alone," Martin said wearily. And Ken said, "Clear off, Haines. We're trying to have a game here."

The three faced him. Bert strutted. "Who are you telling to clear off?"

But Ken wasn't intimidated and Lennie could see that it was only a gesture, a show of strength before they drifted away.

The bell clanged for the end of break.

"You don't want to let Bert Haines push you around," said Ken, sorting the cards and handing Lennie's back to him.

But how do I stop him? thought Lennie. How is it that Ken can tell Bert Haines to clear off when I can't even look at him without getting a fist in my face?

By dinner time everyone knew about Lennie's friend, and there was speculation about who he was. The girls, normally a species apart who despised anything of concern to boys, picked up on the mystery and gave it their full attention. They whispered together during the handwriting lesson; suspicions were exchanged, gossip passed on. "I've *seen* him with Lennie. It's him, honest." "Never!"

"It is." A rumour began to circulate: he's old Wilding's son.

Lennie kept his head low. How did they know? Why did girls always know things like that?

By home time Lennie had scarcely a friend in the school yard. Nearly all the children at the chapel school were from miners' families. "Stuck-up," the girls said, tossing their hair. "Thinks he's better than us." The boys were more imaginative: "Toad." "Creep." "Arse-licker." And, not the most appropriate word but the worst they knew, "Scab."

Scab. Lennie was mortified. No one in his family had ever been called that before. A feeling of disaster overwhelmed him. What had he done? He'd just met Ralph by accident. It was all an accident. It had been bad enough at home, everyone talking about it. Even Mary had said, "You don't want to get mixed up with that sort." Mary, who usually took his part.

Now, in the school yard, he turned to his accusers. "I just met him. I didn't know who he was."

"Thought he was a miner, did you?" sneered Bert. "Sounds like one, doesn't he?"

And Reggie said, "We'll get you, Dyer."

Margaret Palmer mentioned last Sunday's

70

sermon, when the Reverend Sinclair had preached the brotherhood of man and spoken out against Hitler and the fascists in Britain who were stirring up trouble against the Jews.

"Dyer's not a Jew, he's a scab," yelled Bert.

But a few others, who didn't know what a Jew was, latched eagerly on to the new word and shouted, "Jew! Jew!" at Lennie.

"I'm telling Miss," said Margaret Palmer.

And Lennie knew she would. So tomorrow would be worse than today.

Mum was at the sink, peeling carrots.

Lennie hung up his coat without a word.

"What's up with you?"

"Nothing." Lennie kept his head down.

She turned round. "Are those boys picking on you again?"

"No!" said Lennie, too loudly.

He went into the front room and got out his tin from behind the settee. Inside was the message he had taken yesterday from under Blue Cloud's ring. He scuttled upstairs to his space on the landing to read it again.

Ralph's note was on a torn-off piece of school's

headed notepaper. Lennie smoothed it out. It gave the address in fine black copperplate: *Glaydon Manor School, Burwood, near Cheltenham, Glos. Headmaster: Mr J. A. H. Rolleson, BA, MA, Ph.D.* And underneath, a pencilled message: "Released Blue Cloud 10.23 a.m. 31.10.37. Write to me. Ralph."

Write to me. Yesterday had been such a good day, helping Dad tidy the loft, feeding and tending the birds, and every so often stopping to watch the sky for Blue Cloud.

By midday he had been getting anxious. But then, from nowhere it seemed, a whirr of wings, a dark shape dropping down, wings folded, and she was home. He had gone into the loft, caught and calmed her, pulled the twist of paper from under her ring.

Write to me. Lennie had been full of enthusiasm. He'd wanted to write straight away: "Received Blue Cloud." But there was no writing paper in the house, only opened-out backs of envelopes. He couldn't write to Glaydon Manor School on one of those. There were no stamps either. He'd have to wait till Monday.

And now Monday had come and he didn't want to write. Ralph was no good for him. It had made things worse having Ralph for a friend. Mary was right. He should have stuck to his own.

Chapter Nine

Lennie woke up next morning with a pain in his stomach like an iron ball. He didn't want any breakfast.

"You must eat before you go to school," said Mum.

"I don't want to go to school. I don't feel well."

Dad spoke sharply. "You look all right to me."

Lennie knew that Dad thought Mum fussed over him too much. He thought so too but sometimes he wanted her to fuss. He considered his symptoms and felt vague nausea.

"I feel sick as well," he said.

"He does look pale." Mum felt Lennie's forehead. "No fever though. You're not worrying about school, are you? Those boys that bully you?"

"Who's been bullying him?" Dad demanded.

"No one," said Lennie.

"I know they have," said Mum. "Doreen said. Bert Haines and his mates."

"That idiot!" said Dad scornfully. "You don't want to be scared of him, Lennie."

"I'm not," insisted Lennie. "I just don't feel well. I think I might have food poisoning."

"Food poisoning!"

Mum looked offended and Lennie realized he'd said the wrong thing.

"Well, it might be dysentery." He'd read about dysentery somewhere.

Dad burst out laughing. "It's anxiety you've got, Lennie. And you'll only get over it by going in and confronting those bullies."

Lennie toyed with his cereal.

"Maybe he should have a day off," Mum wavered. "He's not strong."

"You let him stay off and it'll be worse for him when he goes back," said Dad. "You know I'm right, Lina. If there's anything really wrong with him they'll send him home."

So Lennie was dispatched, breakfast-less. His mother called out anxiously, "Don't forget your coat."

Lennie walked slowly. The pain dragged at his stomach.

Two doors along, Mrs Richards had a thick privet hedge bordering her garden. Lennie took off his coat and dropped it down between the hedge and the wall. He'd collect it on the way home.

The way home – half past three. It felt like the other side of a mountain he had to climb.

Margaret Palmer must have told the headmaster about Lennie's problems because Mr Walters made a warning speech in assembly about bullying. He didn't mention Lennie by name, and he wrapped it all up in a lot of stuff about tolerance and fair play and the things that were going on in Nazi Germany because bullies had got the upper hand; but everyone knew it was a warning to Bert and his mates to behave themselves – at least in school.

At break time Mr Walters patrolled the yard, and at home time he stood by the gate, staring down the road towards the Red Lion, giving Lennie time to run past.

Lennie was safe. But he didn't feel safe. He felt

singled out, different, and he wanted to be the same as everyone else. The pain in his stomach persisted all week.

Miss Neale made things worse, noticing him. When they had Art she showed the class his painting and pinned it on the wall. All through his time at school Lennie had never let on that he knew the answer to anything, never put his hand up or looked keen. But Miss Neale would try to draw him out. "Lennie, now I'm sure *you* know."

Sometimes he longed for the return of Miss Lidiard, who had found him irritating and had constantly snapped at him to sit up and pay attention.

On Friday a letter came from Ralph: "Did Blue Cloud get home safely? I've been waiting for you to write…"

Lennie felt guilty. Ralph was his friend; he should have written to him. And yet … he wanted so much to be one of the crowd at school.

He went off reluctantly that morning, but it turned out to be a better day. For one thing, it was Guy Fawkes Night and everyone was talking about the bonfire that had been built on the Rough; there would be fireworks, and potatoes baked in the embers. And then there was talk of the pantomime. The headmaster made the announcement in assembly. The school would be putting on a performance of *Cinderella* in January. Miss Quimby was in charge. Everyone was to have a part; the little children would be fairies or mice; the older ones would have the leading parts. There was too much to talk about for anyone to have time to torment Lennie. He ran home unscathed.

Doreen was there, pirouetting on the hearthrug; she had already decided that she wanted to be a fairy.

"Daft," said Lennie, and retreated to the front room. When he emerged at tea time Phyl was washing her hair in the sink and Mary had gone for fish and chips. Dad was writing, papers spread out over the table.

"You'd better get all this cleared away now, Tom," Mum was saying, a mixture of pride and irritation in her voice. "Pit-head baths," she explained to Lennie. "A bit late for us. We could do with a bath here, though."

"We've got one," said Dad. "Hanging on the wall out back."

"No. I mean a bathroom. A proper bath where the water drains away. Where Phyl could wash her hair without dripping all over the kitchen. And an inside privy. Mrs Miller, that I take in sewing for, she's having a bathroom put in. I'd like that, if we had the money. Mary says that if there's a war there'll be jobs for married women. Real jobs, in factories and that."

Dad looked up. "You don't want to work in a factory, Lina? Making weapons. You don't want a war?"

Mum looked shamefaced. "I suppose not. But it'd be a change, wouldn't it, from taking in mending?"

"Will there be a war, Dad?" Lennie asked.

There was always talk of war these days, on the radio, in the papers, even at home. And they'd had a gas mask drill at school last term.

Before Dad could reply, the back door opened and in came Mary, carrying a bag full of warm fragrant newspaper packages which she unloaded on the table.

"Make the most of it," she said, as the family crowded around. "We might be coming out soon."

"What? Oh, Mary! Not a strike!" Mum protested. "Not with your dad off sick."

"It isn't up to me. It's the Union. Management won't back down. They're planning to cut wages all round – just before Christmas, too."

"And my birthday, next week." Doreen's voice was strident. She wanted roller skates.

"Don't worry about your birthday, love," said Phyl. "I'm still in work, Mum. We won't starve."

"I'm not taking your wages."

Mum always refused to take money from Phyl. Phyl was engaged and supposed to be saving for her future.

"You might have to," said Phyl.

Doreen was wriggling on her chair, eager to regain her parents' attention. She jumped in as soon as Phyl stopped talking. "Me and Lennie, we need our pocket money. So we can buy some fireworks to take to the Rough."

Mum smiled and went to get her purse. "Here you are." She put down fourpence for Lennie and twopence halfpenny for Doreen. Doreen pocketed her share quickly and began chattering about fireworks. Lennie didn't listen. He was mentally dividing up his fourpence. He wouldn't buy a comic this week; that way he could buy more fireworks.

So there was a halfpenny for sweets, twopence for fireworks – and a penny halfpenny for a stamp. Because when they came home after the bonfire he was going to write to Ralph.

Chapter Ten

Lennie wrote Ralph a long letter. He told him about
Guy Fawkes Night, the bonfire and the fireworks,
and how someone had posted a banger through Mrs
Lloyd's letter box and she had called the police. He
told him about the preparations for the pantomime,
but nothing else about school; he didn't want Ralph
to know about the gang picking on him and how
scared he felt going in every morning.

He waited eagerly for Ralph's reply, but when it
came he was disappointed. Ralph had enjoyed
Lennie's letter – he urged him to write again soon –
but his own letter was brief, breezy, somehow
unsatisfying.

A fortnight later Mary came out on strike. On

the Friday night Mum told Lennie and Doreen, "We'll go down and support the pickets tomorrow. Take some hot food."

They went on the bus. As it neared the factory Mum began organizing parcels: "Lennie, you take the apple pies. I've got the soup. Doreen! Don't go skipping off, miss. You can carry the bread."

"Can I ring the bell?"

"Yes. Ring it now."

Doreen reached up and pressed the bell. The bus slowed to a halt.

"Lang's Tile Works," the conductor called. He winked at Mum. "They're in good voice."

Even from inside the bus you could hear the shouting and see banners and placards jigging about.

Mum said proudly, "My daughter's on the picket line."

They clambered down the steps with their packages.

The shouting became more distinct as they walked along the road. It was lunch time, and some part-timers who wouldn't join the strike were going in.

"Scab!" "Blackleg!" the pickets yelled, and the offenders had to push their way through the crowd, using their bicycles as protection.

The pickets set up a chant: "No cuts for Christmas! No cuts for Christmas!"

The chanting became a cheer as Mum, Lennie and Doreen arrived.

Mary came forward. Her lips were blue, but Lennie could feel the excitement radiating from her; she loved a fight.

"You're cold, Mary." Mum made an accusation of it.

"I'm all right. What have you brought?"

"Apple pies," said Doreen. "Aunty Elsie made them."

"And soup and bread," said Mum.

"Two flasks! I'll call the girls."

Mary's workmates from the press shop propped their banners against the fence and crowded round – Alice, Kath, Edna, Big Joan and Little Joan. "Soup! Oh, you're wonderful, Mrs Dyer!"

"Just practice," said Mum, pouring soup into mugs. "I seem to have spent my life taking soup to picket lines."

Several families had come with food, making a party atmosphere around the works entrance. Braziers full of red-hot coals were burning, and some men were frying sausages. But the weather was cold – raw and windy, with flurries of sleet. Caps were pulled low over faces, headscarves tied tight. The pickets stamped their feet to keep warm, and Mary complained, "My jaw's that stiff, I can't shout."

"You weren't doing too bad just now," said Mum. "It's not solid, then, the strike?"

"They're trickling back. It's the cold; and Christmas coming…"

Doreen nudged Lennie. Jimmy Morris was offering them sausages. Lennie took one. It was charred on the outside, but when he bit into it the inside was pink. It burned his mouth but he didn't care.

"Want a tater?" Jimmy was pulling baked potatoes out of the fire.

They nodded, their mouths full of sausage.

"Here. Give one to your mum, too."

The food kept them warm for a while. But later, walking home uphill, with the sleet stinging his face, Lennie began to feel martyred, especially when the bus went by, hissing on the wet road.

"We can't afford it both ways," Mum had said.

Lennie could feel the wet seeping in through the soles of his shoes.

"My shoes leak," he said.

"There's a jumble sale at Trinity Hall next week," said Mum. "We'll have to see what we can find. Doreen needs shoes, too. And a longer frock."

"And you need gloves," said Lennie.

Mum's gloves were in holes. She always knitted them for the family but hadn't got around to her own yet.

"I know. I've got chilblains already."

Doreen jumped up and down to get her mother's attention. "I need a fairy dress."

"Aunty Elsie will make that," promised Mum. "She'll enjoy doing it."

"And a wand," sang Doreen. "And wings."

She flapped her arms and ran along the path ahead of them.

"Fly away! And stay there!" Lennie shouted. He said to Mum, "I'm fed up with her being a fairy."

Mum laughed. "*I'd* have flown away if she hadn't got that part. And what about you, Lennie? Doreen says you're a footman or something?"

"Second footman," said Lennie.

It was the sort of part he'd known he would get. Non-speaking. Nothing to do, really, except walk around behind the prince, feeling stupid. Even before Miss Quimby made the announcements, Lennie could have guessed who would get which parts. Ken Forton was the prince; pretty Sylvia Lee was Cinderella; Margaret Palmer was the fairy godmother; Bert Haines and Reggie Dean were the horse.

Back end of the horse – that was the sort of part Lennie would have liked. Unseen but powerful. Well. He was stuck with second footman and Miss Quimby's nagging: "Come on, Lennie, look lively." "Head up, Lennie. *Try* not to look so vacant."

"Rehearsals on Monday," he told Mum gloomily.

And gloomily, on Monday, he went to school.

At first it was as bad as he had expected. Sitting about, watching, while other people forgot their lines and missed their cues; having to sing in the choruses; being chivvied by Miss Quimby. Then they started on the scene where the prince visited Cinderella's house with the lost slipper; and Lennie, attending the prince, and trying to keep his head up as instructed, tripped over a fold of curtain, lurched across the stage, and collided with an ugly sister. A ripple of delight ran through the watching children. "Lennie!" exclaimed Miss Quimby, exasperated.

Lennie was embarrassed; but he saw, in that moment, the possibilities of his role. When they replayed the scene he did an impression of a clumsy yokel, bumping into the prince, and standing about deliberately looking vacant. "Lennie?" Miss Quimby began, but the audience rocked with laughter, and she let it go.

The next rehearsal was on Thursday. By then Lennie had decided that the second footman's problems were due to drink. He staggered about in imitation of Freddie Lloyd leaving the Red Lion on a Saturday night. The audience loved it. Miss Quimby permitted a smile to cross her face. She said, "Just a hint, Lennie. Don't overdo it." On the following Monday he staggered less dramatically but added a discreet hiccup.

After rehearsals started, things began to change for Lennie. The gang bothered him less; other children acknowledged him in the street; he still wasn't any good at football and got caught in "tag", but it didn't seem to matter so much. One day, as they filed silently into school after the break, Martin Reid nudged him and said, "Hic!"

Lennie wrote to Ralph about the pantomime. Ralph wrote back, but not often, and his letters were always short. Then, at the beginning of December, he told Lennie, "Term ends next week. I'll be home on Friday the tenth. See you on the Saturday? Usual place."

The tenth. A whole week before Lennie's school. That could mean trouble. Lennie knew he would never get to meet Ralph after school without someone finding out, and then those new fragile links with his classmates could be broken.

He didn't want to break them. And yet he had to see Ralph. Ralph was his friend.

Chapter Eleven

"Hello."

"Hi."

Lennie tried to sound cool, like someone in an American film.

Ralph was crouching by the fire he had lit in the ruined cottage. He stood up.

"Quite a blaze."

He held out his hands over the fire.

The two boys regarded each other awkwardly. Lennie was aware all over again, after so many weeks without seeing him, of how different Ralph was. It wasn't just the clothes. There was a healthy bloom about him that you never saw in Culverton boys. Lennie knew Ralph must be looking at him and thinking about the differences – the thin darned jersey, the dustiness.

The dust got everywhere in Culverton: black dust from the mines, white dust from the tile and china works, ash from the foundries. The women said their washing came in dirtier than it went out. Lennie thought of the dust that had settled on his dad's lungs over the years until it formed a hard, unshifting layer.

"My dad's dying of the dust," he said.

Ralph looked startled. "Dying? Your father?"

"I don't mean he's dying this minute." Lennie hadn't meant to talk about the dust, hadn't consciously thought until this moment that the dust would eventually kill his father, but it pleased him to have got a reaction. "I mean it's the dust that will kill him, slowly. Like our Uncle Charley. He died of the dust. In the end they just can't breathe. My dad's trying to get compensation from your dad. Didn't you know?"

Ralph stared. "I know who he is now – your father. The Union secretary?"

Lennie nodded.

"Damned smart alec, my father calls him.

Always stirring. A troublemaker. You never told me it was him."

Lennie's fists clenched.

"*You* never told me your dad was George Wilding!"

"You knew!"

"I didn't."

"You're stupid, then. Everyone knows us."

Lennie mocked: "Everyone knows us. Think you're so important, don't you?"

"My father *is* important. He keeps this town employed. Wilding, Denton, Lang – there would be nothing here without the three of them, my father says."

Lennie withdrew a step. How could he ever have liked Ralph? He was one of Them, the bosses. You could hear it in his voice.

Ralph said, uncertainly, "Why are we arguing? It doesn't stop us being friends, does it, what our fathers think of each other?"

Lennie caught a hint of anxiety in his voice, and realized that he, Lennie, had the upper hand for once; it was a new feeling and he enjoyed it.

"Us working folk have to stick together," he said.

It sounded unreal, like something said at a political meeting.

Ralph stared at the fire for a moment. Then he looked up and grinned. "No," he said, "us *two* have to stick together. Against fathers. And families."

Lennie caught the change of mood. "Against sisters."

"Definitely against sisters. Against school."

Against bullies, thought Lennie, but didn't say it.

"Against masters," said Ralph. He began laughing. "Against school dinners. Against cabbage. Against ... against..."

"Against smelly socks," said Lennie. They staggered together, laughing uncontrollably.

"Come over to Old Works?" suggested Lennie. You haven't been there, have you?"

"What is it?"

"Old broken walls. Shafts and that." They ran, talking in gasps. Their breath hung on the cold air.

"I liked your letters," said Ralph.

"You didn't say much in yours."

"Couldn't. The Censor."

"The what?"

"The Deputy Head. All our letters are read before they post them."

Lennie stared. "Can't you post your own?"

"Difficult. Chaps do manage it, of course. Especially the older ones."

"But why...?"

"Tale bearing. Mutiny in the ranks. Can't have that. We can't have Mummy finding out that the food is terrible or that little Johnny's crying himself to sleep every night."

"And do you – they?"

"Oh, it's not too bad. But it can be hard at first."

"I wouldn't like it." Lennie couldn't bear to think of spending weeks, months, away from home; he'd miss his family, even Doreen.

"No danger of *my* father taking me away, of course," said Ralph. "Whether I was happy or not." He laughed. "Some chaps deliberately write long letters for the benefit of the Censor – pages and pages, utterly, totally, catastrophically *boring*."

They had Old Works to themselves. Lennie had calculated that they would; there was a craze for football at the moment, and those who weren't at Saturday morning pictures would be kicking a ball around in the field behind the Rose and Crown.

They climbed on the broken walls and walked a little way into a tunnel that Lennie said was supposed to come out at Springhill.

"Have you been through?"

"No. It gets low, and narrow."

"We could go through. Let's try."

But the tunnel twisted, and as the roof came down lower and lower, forcing them to crouch, they retreated and went back to clambering over the walls and exploring the ruined buildings.

"We could race back to the cottage," said Lennie. He was getting cold. He'd sneaked out without his coat.

But the fire at the cottage had gone out, and it took a long time to relight it. At last Lennie held his cold hands over the flames.

"You'll get chilblains, doing that."

"You should see my mum's hands. She's got awful chilblains. She needs some new gloves. Her old pair's all holey, like."

"Does she only have one pair?"

Lennie was astonished. "Yes!"

"My mother's got pairs and pairs of gloves," said

Ralph. He shivered. "It *is* cold. Do you want to come to our house?"

Lennie thought of the warm carpeted rooms, the books and games. But he shook his head. "Your parents won't like it."

"They're out."

"Mrs Martin, then."

"Mrs Martin is an employee. It's none of her business."

"I feel funny there," said Lennie.

And he knew he would feel funny if Ralph came to *his* house, even though in a way he wanted him to.

They shared Ralph's lunch – soup in a vacuum flask, and sandwiches.

"I can't come tomorrow morning," Ralph said. "There's church; and then we're out visiting."

"And I'm at Aunty Elsie's in the afternoon."

"Monday, then."

"Not till late. Some of us are still at school. You're lucky."

"I'm not. My father will probably take me to the works again – I don't know which days. But I'll come when I can, after school's out."

"I'll bring your book – the King Arthur."

"And I'll bring a torch."

"We could be ghosts in the dark!"

"Yes. Splendid."

It was Wednesday before they met up again. On Monday Lennie had a rehearsal after school and on Tuesday he went to the cottage but Ralph wasn't there. It was cold. The wind cut through his clothes, even through the coat that Mum had insisted he wear. The fire wouldn't light and the autumn leaves had turned to mush. By half past four it was pitch dark. He went home.

But on Wednesday Ralph was waiting for him. He had brought his torch. They took turns to hide in the woods, playing Dicky-shine-a-light and ghosts. Then they started the fire with paper Ralph had brought, and lit a cigarette from it. The December dusk closed in on them as they sat puffing and talking. The fire devoured the paper, and went out, leaving a pile of blackened fragments.

"It's too damp for fires now," said Lennie.

When the flames were leaping it had felt cosy, safe from the crowding trees, but now the cold crept back.

Lennie jumped up and flapped his arms.

"There's a fair going up in the Canal Field," he said. "We seen them putting up the rides and that. Friday it starts."

"Are you going?"

"I might. If I can get round Mum or Phyl to give me some money. Will you go?"

"I'd like to. I'd have to try and sneak out."

"Wouldn't they let you go?"

"I doubt whether my father would think it was suitable."

"Oh. See you tomorrow, anyway?"

"Yes. Oh! I nearly forgot." Ralph felt in his coat pocket and handed Lennie something soft and pliable.

"What is it? Shine the torch."

Lennie found he was holding a pair of leather gloves.

"They're for your mother. You said her gloves were in holes."

"But where did you get these?"

"My mother. She's got plenty of gloves. Those are old ones."

"They don't look old." Lennie put one on. The

inside was lined with silky fur. "I can't give her these."

"Why not?" Ralph's voice, in the darkness, was disappointed. "Won't she like them?"

"Yes, but – well, they're so – I mean, she usually has knitted ones, like. She makes them, or Aunty Elsie does. And – well, they're your mother's."

"She said you could have them. You might as well. Say you bought them – a Christmas present."

"She'd know I couldn't buy anything like this."

"They're just old gloves," said Ralph crossly. "I thought you'd be pleased."

"I am," said Lennie, contrite. "Thank you."

"See you tomorrow, then? Same place, same time?"

"Yes," said Lennie, wishing they could meet somewhere warmer, indoors.

Well, Friday was the first day of the fair. That would be warmer, more cheerful. Perhaps Ralph would come. And as he thought that, Lennie realized that he wasn't sure he wanted him to. Everyone – all the boys from school – would be there.

Chapter Twelve

Lennie didn't give the gloves to Mum. He felt sure, somehow, that she wouldn't want them. All day on Thursday he carried them around in his pockets until Dad said, "What's that you've got, Lennie, a couple of ferrets?" and then he hid them behind the settee with his treasures.

On Friday night he went to the fair.

Mum gave him some money. "There's sixpence each, and a penny between you for sweets."

"Do I *have* to take Doreen?"

"Do you want to go or not?"

Lennie resolved to think of Doreen as six and a half extra pennies in his pocket.

Doreen came downstairs wearing new socks, bright white.

"What are you wearing those for?" Mum demanded.

The socks had been a present from Aunty Elsie for Doreen's birthday; they were so wondrously white and new that until now Mum had permitted Doreen to wear them only when they went to Elsie's for tea.

Doreen stuck out her lower lip.

"You're not wearing those at the fair," Mum insisted. "Go and get your fawn ones."

"Don't *like* them!" Doreen's chin trembled.

"You won't like those if they get covered in mud. Get your old ones. Now!"

Doreen flounced across the room and stomped upstairs.

"That one should be on the stage," said Mum. "Now, look after her, won't you, Lennie? And keep your coats on – it's bitter out. Look, put this scarf round—"

"No!" protested Lennie, twisting away.

"Oh, between the two of you – now here's Phyl wanting her tea."

Phyl came in pink from the cold. She was warming her hands at the fire when Doreen reappeared, in fawn socks, and began explaining her troubles.

Phyl comforted her. "They won't show in the dark."

She gave Lennie and Doreen another sixpence each. Lennie glowed. They could go on several rides now – the dodgems, the ghost train – *and* have sweets. They might even be able to afford the big wheel if Doreen didn't want to go on too many of the baby roundabouts...

Outside, it was dark. Frost sparkled on the pavement. Doreen skipped and twirled, practising her fairy dance. Lennie saw some older children coming. "Leave off," he hissed.

He held on to her hand as they entered the fair. He didn't want to, but he knew he'd get hell from Mum if he lost her, and Doreen was such a little devil for getting her own way.

People pressed around them, dark, anonymous in their winter coats. Red and gold bulbs flicked on and off around the booths, jangling music came from the roundabouts; screams, laughter, music called them this way and that.

"I want to go on the bus one," Doreen said,

pulling Lennie's hand. "Lennie, I want—"

"In a minute."

What Lennie wanted first was to wander around, looking and listening, feeling the atmosphere. He didn't want to be rushed onto Doreen's choice of roundabout. He wanted to take it slowly, plan what to spend his shilling on.

There were booths with rifles and targets; a clairvoyant; a Ferris wheel turning slowly against the night sky; a stall where you threw hoops and could win teddy bears, purses, key rings.

"Lennie, do this one. Lennie, I want a teddy. Lennie…"

So insistent was Doreen's that at first Lennie didn't hear the other voice behind him. "Lennie! Lennie!"

Then he turned round and saw Ralph.

Ralph said, "I managed to give everyone the slip. Have to be back for dinner, though."

Dinner. Lennie could smell hot pies, and his tea had worn off already. But the pies were expensive; they didn't come into his financial planning.

He said, apologetically, "I had to bring Doreen."

"That's all right. Hello, Doreen."

Doreen sparkled. She was not used to being acknowledged by Lennie's friends.

Ralph turned to Lennie. "Guess what I've got?"

"What?"

Ralph put his hand in his pocket and pulled out coins. Not sixpences. Big, heavy coins. Four half-crowns.

Lennie stared. "That's ten shillings! Ten shillings for the fair? But you said your father wouldn't let you go?"

Ralph looked away.

"Where did you get it?"

"It's mine. Pocket money, saved up." He gave two half-crowns to Lennie. "Two each."

"Pocket money?" said Lennie.

He wasn't sure he believed Ralph. But who cared? With five shillings each they could go on everything. They could have their fortune told and go on the ghost train and buy candyfloss for Doreen. Phyl's hard-earned sixpences seemed irrelevant now.

As they made their way to the dodgems, Lennie felt a twinge of regret for the loss of the need to consider and choose, but it soon passed, and they climbed into the cars, Ralph in one, Lennie and Doreen in another. The power came on, the contacts sparked on the roof and Lennie felt his car jerk and move. Doreen squealed as they were rammed from behind and Lennie spun the steering wheel to weave a way between the other cars and crash sideways into Ralph.

Ralph was struggling. He obviously hadn't had much practice – probably none, knowing old Wilding. Lennie felt superior as he boxed him in and rammed him repeatedly from side, front and rear.

They stayed in the cars for another go, although Doreen was talking hopefully about roundabouts. This time Ralph steered better, and they got out into the mainstream and were separated. Lennie felt a sudden violent bump from behind, turned, and saw Bert and Alan leering at him. They rammed him again.

"I don't *like* it, Lennie," said Doreen.

She cringed as another violent collision sent them into the car in front.

When the cars stopped, Lennie got Doreen out quickly and looked round for Ralph. "Can we go on the roundabout now – the bus one?" Doreen asked.

She took Lennie's hand and clung tightly. He could feel her fear.

"All right."

Ralph joined them as they moved towards the roundabout. Lennie saw with relief that Bert and Alan were still on the dodgems. But they were watching him; they had recognized Ralph.

Lennie put Doreen on the ride and went with Ralph to a nearby booth and threw plastic hoops for prizes. Ralph won a ring with a green stone in it. When Doreen came off the roundabout he gave it to her. Doreen was enthralled. She wore it on her thumb all evening, turning it often to admire the way it caught the light.

Ralph and Lennie bought hot pies. Doreen was in an agony of indecision over whether to have a pie or candyfloss.

"Have both," Ralph suggested.

Doreen did, and felt sick.

They saw Phyl and her fiancé, Jim; and Mary and some friends from work, all screaming on the big dipper. Everyone from school was there; every-one saw Lennie with Ralph, going on ride after ride, eating pies, playing the rifle range and the hoop-la.

And then Ralph asked someone the time, and exclaimed, "I'll have to go. Lennie, come to my house tomorrow afternoon. It's too cold in the woods."

"Your parents—" Lennie began.

"They're going out. If you're worried about Mrs Martin, just come to the back garden gate. I'll look out for you. Agreed?"

"All right."

"Good. About two? See you!"

Ralph ran off through the crowd, leaving Lennie still with change from his five shillings and Doreen saying, "I might feel not so sick if I had some sweets. Lennie, Mum said we could have sweets…"

They went home, sucking sherbet through liquorice straws.

Mum was ironing when they got in, and Dad was in his chair by the fire, reading a newspaper.

"I've got a ring! Look!" said Doreen. And before Lennie could stop her she had told them about Ralph having ten shillings to spend and giving five to Lennie.

"Ten shillings!" exclaimed Dad, frowning. And Mum said, "They must have money to burn, those people. You didn't need the money I gave you, then?"

She was hurt, as Lennie had known she would be. When she had gone upstairs to put a hot-water bottle in Doreen's bed, he turned on Doreen and said, "You're so *stupid*."

Doreen didn't understand. Her eyes filled with tears, and Lennie felt mean.

Later, when Doreen had gone to bed, Lennie counted up the coins he had left. He found his mother folding clothes in her bedroom. She looked unhappy. He put the money on the dressing table.

"What's that?"

"Change. Two and eight."

"That's yours. Keep it."

"I'm giving it to you."

She hesitated, then swept the coins into her hand.

He turned to go.

"Lennie!"

He looked back.

"Come in and shut the door. Now Doreen's out of the way, you've got some explaining to do."

Lennie felt a flutter of guilt. What had he done?

She opened the drawer and took out a pair of gloves – the gloves he had hidden under the settee.

"I was cleaning the front room," she said.

Lennie's dismay was mingled with a release of tension. It had been preying on his mind – what he should do with the gloves.

"They were a secret – " he began, stammering. "Christmas—"

"Where did you get them?"

"Ralph—"

"Ralph gave them to you?" Her face cleared, and he realized that she had been afraid he had stolen them. He flushed with indignation.

"What did you think?" he demanded.

"I didn't know what to think." She rounded on him again. "So what have you been saying to Ralph? Do those people think we can't afford gloves? You know I'm knitting some – nearly finished. What have you said?"

"Nothing. I – I don't know. I might have – Ralph says he asked his mother; she said you could have them. I think Ralph meant to help…"

Mum's face softened. "I'm sure he did. But they're much too good, Lennie. Look at them."

She drew one on, and held out her hand, wistfully. The glove was black, made of fine soft leather, with decorative tucks along the back and fingers and a tiny button loop at the wrist.

"It suits you," said Lennie.

"They look so new," she said. "Not stretched or wrinkled. Did Mrs Wilding really say Ralph could give them to you?"

She looked at him searchingly, and Lennie felt himself blushing. He thought of the ten shillings Ralph had brought to the fair, and remembered him taking cigarettes from the hall table and saying, "Finders keepers."

I don't trust Ralph, he thought. He didn't like to admit it, but it was true.

"You must take them back," said Mum.

Lennie exclaimed, "I can't! And if she *did* say—"

"Even if she did. You must tell them we can't accept them. They're too good. It's not right."

Lennie stared miserably at a crack in the lino.

"We've got our pride, you know," Mum said, gently. "And besides, we're not that poor. Dad's back at work now, and the strike's over at Lang's; Mary says they're going back Monday."

Lennie saw a chance to change the subject.

"Did they win?"

"Of course not. They've compromised. Not such a big cut, and a review promised in the spring. Dad says that's the best they could expect."

"Oh."

"When are you seeing Ralph?" Mum asked.

"Tomorrow."

"Take them back tomorrow, then?"

He shuffled his feet. "All right."

"Promise?"

Lennie looked up. He said angrily, "I promise! I'm not a liar. Only – Ralph will feel—"

"Offended? Not if you're tactful."

Tactful. Only grown-ups knew about being tactful, Lennie thought.

"There's another thing," Mum said.

He looked up, surly. "What?"

She smiled. "That squashed frog behind the settee. Get rid of it before Elsie comes at Christmas. Please."

Chapter Thirteen

Lennie stood halfway down the wooded slope above the Wildings' house, looking through bare branches at the twisted chimney-pots, the tennis court and the lawn with a layer of frost on it. The gloves were stuffed into his right-hand trouser pocket.

Wait by the garden gate, Ralph had said.

Lennie scrambled down, unwillingly. He wanted to see Ralph, but he didn't want to give the gloves back. He dreaded explaining, being tactful. Mum had told him what to say: "It's very kind of you; she appreciates the thought." But he still wished the gloves would disappear of their own accord, relieving him of the need to say anything at all.

Ralph's window was blank, a net curtain across

the lower half. In a moment Ralph would see him through the net; perhaps he was already on his way downstairs.

But the back door stayed shut.

Lennie stamped his feet impatiently. He was cold.

He stared at Ralph's window. It must be gone two o'clock, he thought. He had left home at half past one, and it was a fair walk to Love Lane. Perhaps Ralph was in the kitchen, having *his* dinner – no, lunch.

He paced up and down beside the fence, willing Ralph to come out, get it over with, so that things could be back to normal between them.

Perhaps Ralph had forgotten? Or didn't know the time? That house was full of clocks, but perhaps there wasn't one in Ralph's room. Or it had stopped.

Lennie swung his arms about and stamped. Surely Ralph should have seen him by now if he was looking out?

He tried calling, "Ralph!" but he was too far away to be heard.

He stared at the house, and the house seemed to stare back indifferently, with blank windows and closed doors.

I'll go and knock, Lennie thought. After all, he'd been invited. There was no need to be afraid of Mrs Martin.

And yet, as he opened the gate, his heart began to beat faster.

His shoes left prints on the frosty grass. There were other prints, he noticed, but not Ralph's – bigger ones; and a wheelbarrow full of leaves and dead branches near the back door. He glanced about, but there was no other sign of the gardener; perhaps he was round at the front.

Lennie reached the back door and knocked tentatively. His knock caused the door to swing open; it had been left unlatched. From behind an inner door he could hear Mrs Martin humming along to music on the wireless. The humming continued unbroken; she hadn't heard him.

He'd have to knock on the inner door. He braced himself to confront her, and stepped into the scullery. On the opposite wall was a row of coats hanging on hooks. One of them, a woman's, had big patch pockets gaping open. Lennie stared at the pockets. An idea came to him.

He could get rid of the gloves, quickly, now, before

he saw Ralph. Put them in a coat pocket and fulfil his promise to Mum without needing to say anything to Ralph. And Mrs Wilding would find them eventually.

Hastily he pulled the gloves out of his own pocket and reached for the coat.

"Got you!"

A hand seized his shoulder and swung him round. Lennie thought his legs would give way with fright. He looked up into the unfriendly whiskered face of the gardener.

"I – I – was calling for Ralph—" he stammered.

But the gardener had seized the gloves from his hands.

"You little devil! I knew you was up to no good when I seen you sneaking in."

"I didn't – I wasn't—"

The realization of how things must look dawned on Lennie as he was propelled by the shoulders into the kitchen. Mrs Martin was jointing a chicken. She looked up, startled, as the gardener announced, with satisfaction, "You'd better get on the telephone to the police, Mrs M. I've just catched this lad stealing a pair of gloves."

Mrs Martin's face hardened. She washed her

hands and switched off the wireless. The gardener handed her the gloves.

"Those are Mrs Wilding's," she said.

"I didn't take them," Lennie protested. "I was bringing them back. I—"

"You were bringing them back but you didn't take them?" Mrs Martin repeated sarcastically.

"No. I mean – Ralph took them – gave them to me. But I thought – I mean my mum said…" Lennie knew he could never explain. "Ask Ralph," he said. "It wasn't me…"

"The family aren't here," said Mrs Martin, "as I've no doubt you knew—"

"I didn't!" Lennie protested. "Ralph told me—"

"Which is why," she continued smoothly, "you took the opportunity to come sneaking round to see what you could lay your hands on. Taking advantage, like all your sort. I knew all along Master Ralph shouldn't be associating with you."

She glanced up at the gardener, and Lennie could see that she had no time for him either. "Leave the boy with me, Reynolds."

The gardener said again, "You ought to ring the police."

"It's not my place to call the police," said Mrs Martin, and Lennie felt a wash of relief go through him. "Mr Wilding will decide whether the police should be called."

The gardener's fingers dug into Lennie's shoulder. He was not to be easily shifted. "You know what I'm thinking, Mrs M?" – Lennie saw her wince at the familiarity – "That ten shillin' that went missing, that was left out to pay the handyman. We was all under suspicion for that – me, and John, and your Stella." He looked darkly at Lennie.

Lennie stared, appalled. What had he walked into? And where was Ralph?

"I never—" he began.

"Thank you, Reynolds," said Mrs Martin. "Leave the boy with me."

The grip on Lennie's shoulder eased and, without thinking, with the instinct of a trapped animal, he broke free and ran, in a hopeless dash for the back door. He collided with the man, who pushed him back into the kitchen, saying, "The police'll deal with you, my lad," and went out, shutting the door.

Mrs Martin went into the scullery, locked the back

door behind Reynolds and pocketed the key. She came back and closed the door into the passage.

Lennie began to cry. "I didn't take them," he wept. "I just wanted to put them back."

"Sit down," said Mrs Martin. She glanced at the clock on the wall. "It's three o'clock. Mr Wilding should be back in an hour or so. You can wait."

Lennie sat down trembling. Mrs Martin continued with her work, coldly oblivious to his snuffles. Stella came in and stared at him. She came closer, touched his wet cheek, and said, "Don't cry." Lennie cringed, hating himself for it.

Mrs Martin drew Stella gently away, found her some washing-up to do and told her not to talk to Lennie.

Lennie stood up and shouted, "I've got to go home! My mum's expecting me."

Stella jumped in fright.

"Your mother will have to wait," said Mrs Martin calmly.

"Where's Ralph?" Lennie demanded. "He told me to meet him here at two o'clock. He *told* me."

He ran to the door into the passage and shouted, "Ralph! Ralph!"

Mrs Martin seized him by the shoulders and sat him down.

"Master Ralph is out," she said.

"Where is he?"

"With his father."

Mrs Martin put the chicken in the oven and began scraping carrots. Stella finished the washing-up and was told to peel potatoes. Lennie listened to Stella's splashings at the sink, the scrape of Mrs Martin's knife, the steady tick tick of the clock.

Four o'clock passed. Half past four.

Mrs Martin produced a piece of paper and a pencil and put them in front of Lennie.

"You'd better write down your name and address."

Lennie wrote it.

"I want to go home," he said, but she ignored him, except to take the paper and put it in her pocket.

"I *have* to go home," Lennie repeated.

He began to shake at the prospect of an interview with Mr Wilding. But at least Ralph would be there. Ralph would explain everything. It would all be sorted out in the end, and Mrs Martin would be proved wrong, and serve her right. He looked with loathing at her neat blonde head bent over the colander. You wait, he thought, you'll look such an idiot when Ralph gets back.

At five o'clock they heard a door slam and voices in the hall. The Wildings were home. Mrs Martin washed her hands and dried them briskly. Lennie sensed her satisfaction. He felt his heart beating so hard that he could scarcely breathe.

"Keep an eye on him," Mrs Martin told Stella, and went out of the room.

Lennie heard her light, accusing voice, and a man's voice answering her. He didn't hear Ralph; perhaps he'd gone upstairs. Then the man said clearly, "Send John. And bring the boy to me." Five minutes later Mrs Martin was back. "Come this way," she ordered Lennie.

Lennie followed her along the passage, through the hall, and into a room he had not entered before – a formal sitting room full of upholstered chairs and gleaming mirrors, with a thick maroon carpet underfoot. The gloves lay on a low table.

Ralph was not there. Only Mr Wilding, standing with his back to the door.

Mrs Martin said, "The boy, sir." She stayed in the room, arms folded and lips pursed.

Mr Wilding turned round.

Lennie saw, with a shock, that he looked like Ralph. Like Ralph, and yet different – this was a hard, stern, uncompromising face. Lennie remembered what Dad and the other men had said about him, how he was fair, but a stickler for the rule book; he worked long hours himself and would grind every last pennyworth of time out of those who worked for him.

Fear made Lennie gabble: "It's not true!" He glanced back at Mrs Martin. "It's not true what she says. You must believe me." And before Mr Wilding could accuse him of anything he launched into a confused explanation of what had happened.

George Wilding listened, unsmiling. He said, "It's bad enough to steal, without inventing stories to cover up your crime. Especially when they implicate others."

The cold legality of his words frightened Lennie. He began to shake.

"Don't call the police," he begged. "Ask Ralph. Ralph knows I didn't take them. Ask Ralph. Please. Ask Ralph."

"Are you trying to suggest that my son stole the gloves—"

"He didn't *steal* them," said Lennie. "He told me his mother said I could have them, for *my* mother, but I – I didn't..." Lennie faltered. He couldn't say, "I didn't believe him." Oh, if only Ralph were here! "Please," he begged, "ask Ralph."

Abruptly George Wilding turned to Mrs Martin. "Fetch my son," he ordered.

Lennie relaxed a little, brushing away tears.

When he heard Ralph's voice outside, his heart leapt and relief flooded through him.

"Ralph!" he exclaimed, as his friend came into the room. "Tell him it wasn't me! Tell him."

"Be quiet," said George Wilding. "Come here, Ralph."

Ralph glanced sidelong at Lennie, then at the gloves on the table. He went obediently to his father's side.

"Ralph, you seem to know this boy."

"Yes, sir." Ralph's voice was a whisper, and Lennie saw that he was afraid of his father.

"How did you come to know him?"

"He plays in the woods, behind the house.

I've met him sometimes."

"I see. And did you give your mother's gloves to this boy?"

Ralph mumbled something.

"Look up, and speak up," ordered his father.

Ralph looked up. He looked at his father, not at Lennie.

"No," he said. "I never gave them to him."

Chapter Fourteen

Lennie didn't care about anything after that. Ralph, passing him as he went out of the room, looked sorry. Lennie glared with brimming eyes.

The door shut behind Ralph. Lennie supposed the police would be called, he'd go to prison, or appear in court in handcuffs, or whatever happened to criminals, but he didn't care. Nothing seemed to matter now.

Mr Wilding said, "You'd better sit down," and sent for a glass of water. Lennie sat gingerly on the edge of one of the big squashy chairs. Mrs Martin handed him the water and he drank it quickly, gasping.

As he put down the glass he heard voices in the hall – several women all speaking at once – and the next moment the door burst open and he saw with amazement his slightly-built mother elbow the larger Mrs Martin out of the way and explode into the room, demanding, "What's this you're saying my Lennie's done?" Behind her came Mary and Phyl, straight from work, Mary shedding clay dust and Phyl with her Woolworths overall showing under her coat.

Lennie gave a sob and ran to his mother.

Mrs Martin turned on Mary: "Coming in here, dropping dust everywhere!"

"You're lucky I haven't come from the pit," retorted Mary. "I'd chuck a ton of soot over this place if I had the chance."

Mum was demanding an explanation from George Wilding. "Who are you to make accusations against my son? What proof have you got?"

"He was caught red-handed," George Wilding replied crisply.

Lennie let go of Mum and began, once again, his complicated explanation. His mother listened, picking up points and turning them on George Wilding like missiles: "He gave them to *me*." "*I* told him to bring them back."

Phyl joined in. "And what about her? Your missus? Have you asked her?"

"My wife is not at home, and in any case I will not have her involved in this affair."

"Oh, listen to him! Seems to me she is involved, like."

"Mrs Dyer," said George Wilding, looking harassed, "I sent for your husband to fetch the boy home. I didn't expect a crowd of unruly women. If you and your daughters don't leave immediately I shall be obliged to call the police."

"Don't worry, we're going," said Mum, pulling Lennie towards her. "And you'll be hearing from my husband, Mr Wilding. He wasn't fit enough to come out here, with his chest being so bad, as you should know, being responsible for it; but you'll be hearing from him, never fear."

"I think the boy has learnt his lesson," said George Wilding mildly. "I'm prepared to overlook this incident on the understanding that he breaks off the association with my son."

"Overlook it!" retorted Mary. "You needn't think—"

"Mary," said Mum. "That's enough. Let's get

Lennie home. He needs his tea."

All the way home, Mum, Mary and Phyl chattered and exclaimed over Lennie's head.

"We told the bugger! And that stuck-up Mrs Martin. I wiped the floor with her."

Phyl laughed. "I think he thought you'd just stand there, Mum, and take it, while he gave you a lecture on child-rearing."

"I love the way he says, 'I don't want my wife involved.'"

"And the dust! Oh, Mary, your clayey shoes all over that carpet! It was a joy to see!"

Lennie couldn't share in their exuberance. He was thinking about Ralph. He had believed that Ralph was his friend, but Ralph had betrayed him.

"You can't trust the nobs. They're no good. They're all the same."

That was Mary's verdict. And Dad's. "Best if people keep to their own sort," he said.

Lennie sat silent, closed in on his misery, while they talked around him. At least they were all on his side; none of them had criticized him, except for having chosen the wrong person for a friend –

and he didn't need telling that.

"What a thing to do, though," said Phyl, who was washing up while Mum dried. "To drop your friend in it to save yourself."

"He was no friend of yours, Lennie," said Mary.

Doreen was sitting on the hearthrug, listening.

"I *liked* Ralph," she said.

Lennie felt a rush of affection for her.

Yes, he thought, so did I.

It was all very well Dad and Mary going on about the bosses and keeping to your own kind; he'd liked Ralph, and Ralph had liked him – surely he had? It wasn't phoney, like Mary said. So why had Ralph caved in and let Lennie take the blame? I wouldn't have done it to him, Lennie thought.

Mum said to Doreen, "Time you were in bed, my girl."

"Oh, Mum!"

"This is none of your business."

"But it's interesting."

"It's all right, Doreen," said Lennie. "I'm going too."

"I'll help you get your bed out, love," said Mum.

"No. I can do it."

It was a relief to go into the front room and shut

the door on the family's concern for him.

He made up the bed and got into it, but sleep would not come. Over and over again his mind replayed the events of the afternoon. Over and over again he heard Ralph say, "No. I never gave them to him." It was dawn before he fell asleep, and yet he woke at his usual time to the sound of his mother riddling the fire in the kitchen.

He got up, packed the bed away, and opened the curtains, letting in a grey cold light. He looked at his reflection in the mirror and was gratified by the pale face and dark-shadowed eyes he saw there. If he'd been wronged, he thought, he might as well look the part.

He pulled out from behind the settee the stack of comics Ralph had given him: *Dandy*, *Beano*, *Hotspur*. From their paper bag he took the complete set of bird cards and the letters Ralph had written him from school. He piled all the things in the middle of the floor.

Mum came in.

"Can I borrow a shopping bag?" Lennie asked.

"Why? What are you up to?"

"Nothing."

"That's no answer. I'm taking Doreen to chapel soon. Why don't you come?"

Lennie looked at her.

She sighed, and brought a hessian shopping bag. Lennie began putting the pile of things into it, aware of her anxious gaze.

He was relieved when she went upstairs to rouse Doreen. Picking up the bag, he left the house, heading for Love Lane.

The cottage was deserted, as he'd known it must be. Ralph was probably under lock and key.

He tore pages from a comic, screwed them up in the fireplace, and put a match to them. They lit instantly. He ripped more pages and fed the fire. Yellow flames leapt up. He watched as Dan Dare turned brown like toast, curled over slowly, blackened and crumpled.

The fire went out. He lit it again, adding branches from the store he and Ralph had made under the window ledge. He fed the flames alternately with sticks and paper until they roared and crackled and made a wall of heat.

He began tearing pages faster and faster, screwing them up and tossing them on the fire. All his anger against Ralph went into the furious ripping and tearing.

He stood back and watched the pyre. It was burning well now, and smoke was rising in a thick column full of ash and paper. He threw on the bird cards and the fire seethed and red worms wriggled in it and red-gold sparks flew upwards. Last of all he burned the letters. Ralph's handwriting showed briefly before slipping into the red heart.

When everything in the bag was gone he crouched by the fire and watched it burn down. The branches were damp, and once the brief flare from the paper was gone the flames died quickly, leaving blackened branches and a pile of powdery black and grey fragments.

Lennie stood up and kicked the ashes, kicked away the stones that formed the hearth, kicked the dead branches. He found his tin by the wood stack. In it were pencils, marbles and conkers. He picked out the marbles he had won from Ralph and hurled them, one by one, into the undergrowth. Then he put the lid on the tin and dropped it into the hessian bag.

He looked around the cottage. He had finished.

He would go home and never come here again.

Love Lane was cold. The bare branches of the trees rattled in a cold wind. A single leaf drifted down, a hazel, pale yellow, perfect, the sort of leaf that invited you to keep it. It lay before him, glowing like sunshine on the path. Deliberately, Lennie trod on it and ground it under his heel.

He walked on. As he approached the Red Lion he heard boys' voices raised in excitement – the football crowd. They had been playing, as usual, in the field behind the Rose and Crown, and were heading home for their dinner.

Lennie shrank from the thought of encountering them. Things had been better at school lately, but he would never be part of this group, and today, especially, he felt isolated. It was too late to turn back; as he reached the wall of the Red Lion's yard – the old ambush place – they swung around the corner into the street and spotted him: Bert Haines, Reggie Dean, Alan Revell, and about a dozen others, whooping and yelling, with muddy knees and hands and faces red with cold.

Lennie tried to slip past, but Bert stopped him. He lolled with his hand against the wall, blocking

Lennie's way. "Here's little Lennie, the bosses' friend!" he said.

"I'm not!" retorted Lennie, with more feeling than usual.

"Been to see your posh friend, have you?" sneered Bert. "Down the woods? *We* know where you go."

"He's not my friend," said Lennie, trying to push past.

Reggie snatched the bag from his hand and shook it upside down. The tin hit the ground and burst open, scattering its contents. Hands began grabbing. Alan got most of the conkers. Someone else pocketed the matches.

"Leave him alone," remonstrated a boy at the back of the crowd. "Don't pinch his stuff." But Lennie saw from the eagerness in most of the faces around him that they were hungry for a fight. He panicked, ducked under Bert's arm, and ran. It was all they needed. They charged after him, yelling, surrounded him, and pinned him against the wall.

Bert stuck his fist under Lennie's nose. "Bosses' friend," he said.

Lennie felt Bert's knuckles bruising his lip and

smelt the earth of the football field. He struggled. "Let me go."

"Had plenty of money to spend at the fair, didn't you?" said Bert. "We saw you, going on all the rides, flashing your money about. Where did you get it, arse-licker?"

"Ralph gave it to me," said Lennie, and immediately wished he hadn't spoken.

"Oh, Walf gave it to him!" said Bert, and the cry was taken up, "Walf! Walf!"

"Walf Wilding!" sniggered Alan.

"Our posh fwend, Walf!"

"He's *not* my friend!" exclaimed Lennie furiously.

Bert pushed his face into Lennie's. "Lennie Dyer is an arse-licker. Say it."

"No!"

Bert seized Lennie's arm and twisted it behind his back. "Say it." He pulled harder, and Lennie winced. "Say it, Dyer."

"No," gasped Lennie.

Bert pushed forward, and Lennie fell on his knees. Before he could get up, Bert had jumped on him and grabbed his hair, pulling his head up. "I said, say it."

Lennie kept silent. He knew that whatever Bert did, he wouldn't say it. Nothing could make him. He might have to die, but he wouldn't say it.

Bert pushed Lennie's face into the dirt. Lennie felt grit in his mouth; a stone cut his lip and he tasted blood.

"Say it!" Bert snarled, pushing down on Lennie's head.

"Say it! Say it! Say it!" chanted the mob.

And while they chanted, Lennie was thinking, desperation sharpening his wits.

He grunted.

"He's saying it!" cried Reggie. "Let's hear him, Bert."

Bert released the pressure.

Lennie lifted his head and brushed stones from his face. "All right," he whispered, licking at a trickle of blood. "I'll say it. Let me get up first."

"Get up, then."

He got to his feet. His legs shook. He drew breath and looked around him, made sure of their attention. Into the waiting silence he said, "Bert Haines is a gorilla."

A ripple of nervous laughter went round the

crowd. Bert's face darkened. Then someone at the back of the crowd jumped up and down, arms dangling, and scratched his armpits. The caricature was taken up and copied, laughter bubbled and broke free, and soon everyone was laughing and play-acting at being a gorilla and making grunting noises and pretending to swing from trees. Alan and Reggie joined in with gusto.

Bert turned on Lennie and hit him. The blow sent him staggering against the wall. A second blow smashed into his cheek and nose and he felt blood flowing fast. Lennie thought, this is it; he'll finish me now. But Bert had lost his supporters. The others called out, "Here, that's enough!" "Give him a chance, Haines." "It's not fair!"

And then a door opened along the street and a woman shouted, "What's going on over there?" and they ran, all of them, Bert included, and Lennie was left wiping the blood from his face and smiling.

Chapter Fifteen

Lennie manoeuvred his bicycle out of the shed and wheeled it down the back garden path. Dad was hoeing between rows of radish and spring greens.

"Off to work?"

"Yes," said Lennie. He had a delivery job at the butcher's now – Saturday mornings and an hour after school. This week, summer half term, he'd been helping out in the shop as well.

He paused by the pigeon loft. "I'll take the young birds out for a toss this afternoon if you like. Martin's taking his out to Hazeley; I said I'd go with him."

"Good idea." Dad was better, but not fit enough for an eight-mile cycle ride; and Mary had a boyfriend; so these days it was usually Lennie who took the birds on the longer tosses.

He wheeled the bicycle out of the gateway and cycled down the lane. The grass verges were bright with dandelions and the air was summer sweet. It was going to be a warm day.

In the High Street he passed Reggie Dean, and called hello. Reggie was all right now; a bit of a dope, but friendly enough. There was no one at school Lennie didn't get on with these days except Bert Haines, and Bert never bothered him any more – he kept out of Lennie's way. Bert had lost his hold over the other boys since the gorilla incident; he had only to start throwing his weight around and someone was sure to be loping about with hunched shoulders. What with that and the school panto-mime, Lennie had gained a reputation as a joker. Growing two inches taller had helped, too.

Martin Reid was outside the grocer's, loading up his bicycle. He did deliveries for Mr Greening.

"Coming this afternoon?" he called.

Lennie's reply was drowned by the shattering roar of a plane, close overhead. Another followed it, then three more in quick succession.

Lennie stopped cycling. People had come out of the shops to stare up at the sky.

"My dad says there's definitely going to be a war," said Martin. "My brother wants to join up."

"So does my sister," said Lennie. "She wants to fly."

"They won't have women flying planes."

"Mary says they will – says they'll have to."

He thought it sounded daft, too. And yet if any girl could get into the Air Force and fly a plane, Mary would.

"I'll come round after dinner," he said, and free-wheeled down to the bottom of the High Street.

Mr Lee, the butcher, was ready with his parcels.

"I'm hoping you can take some extra today, Lennie? Ken's mum just called in; seems he's poorly."

"I don't mind."

"I'll make it worth your while." Mr Lee pushed several parcels to one side. "Those are your usuals. You'd better do those first and then come back. These others are up the top end, mostly – I've written the addresses on; that one's Dale House, Miss Ingram; and that's The Hollies, Mrs Wilding."

"Mrs Wilding?" Lennie's heart began to race.

"Up Bridge Road, Woodend."

"Yes. Yes, I know where it is."

"Good. Off you go, then."

Lennie filled the basket on the front of his bicycle.

Wildings. He was angry with himself for being so disturbed. The incident with the gloves was over, forgotten; no one had done any more about it, not even Dad. Dad said chances were the Wildings knew their son was untrustworthy and guessed Lennie was probably telling the truth. Ralph had written to Lennie after Christmas, saying he was sorry, asking Lennie to write, but Lennie had thrown the letter away. It all seemed a long time ago. Lennie was twelve; he had a job; he had other friends; he had forgotten Ralph – almost.

He left the Hollies till last. It was furthest out, anyway, further by road than it was from the woods off Love Lane. He cycled out of Culverton and along a country road between banks of hazel and wild garlic.

He had never approached the Wildings' house from the front before. As he wheeled his bicycle round the side of the house he saw the gardener bent over a flowerbed and felt his legs trembling. He had to force himself to knock at the familiar back door.

It was a different maid who answered, not Stella. But then there was a query about the price of the sausages, and Mrs Martin had to be called, and Lennie waited in alarm as she came out, wiping her hands on her apron.

She didn't recognize him. After all that had happened Lennie could scarcely believe it. But he was just the butcher's boy, a fair haired boy with a bike; she didn't give him a second glance. He was nothing to these people.

He took the money and wheeled the bicycle around the side of the house. And as he did so the front door opened, he looked up, and saw Ralph coming out, alone.

Ralph started. *He* knew Lennie.

Lennie swung his leg over the crossbar.

"Lennie!" said Ralph. He darted across the lawn and jumped a flowerbed. "Lennie, wait!"

But Lennie pushed hard on the pedals, sped down the drive, and swung out onto Bridge Road.

* * *

Back home, Mum said, "What's up with you? You look ruffled."

"I had to deliver to Wildings. I saw Ralph."

"What did he say?"

"Nothing. Well – he tried to speak to me but I rode off."

Mum began laying the table for dinner. "Oh," she said.

Lennie rounded on her. "You don't expect me to speak to him, do you?"

"It depends what you want."

"I don't want anything to do with him."

And yet Lennie knew that wasn't true. He was angry with Ralph, and hurt, but—

"Mary says I should never have got mixed up with him," he said. "She says the nobs are not like us; they're all cheats and liars. She says they don't have any real feelings; they make use of people like us. That's what she says."

"Mary's young," said Mum. "She doesn't know everything."

"What doesn't she know?"

Tell me, he implored her silently; tell me it wasn't really like that.

Mum said, "Perhaps you should look at it from Ralph's point of view. His father is such a hard, righteous, upright man. And Ralph is afraid of him – you saw that. That's why he let you down, because he was so afraid of his father, not because he didn't care about you. He *did* care. He does."

"But I wouldn't have done it to him, no matter how afraid I was!" Lennie exclaimed. "I *couldn't* have."

"I know that," said Mum. "But Ralph isn't you. People are different. It's harder for him."

Lennie didn't reply, but he felt comforted for the first time since that dreadful day.

And later, on Hazeley Common with Martin, watching the two flocks of pigeons mingle, separate, and fly off towards Culverton, he thought again of Ralph. He remembered the games they had played, the secret codes, the cigarettes they had shared.

Mum had said, "Perhaps you should look at it from Ralph's point of view." How did Ralph feel now? Guilty, unforgiven, left behind in the dark of winter?

Lennie still had the scrap of paper with Ralph's school address on it that had been tucked under

Blue Cloud's ring. It was the only thing he'd kept.

"Write to me," Ralph had said.

Perhaps I will, Lennie thought.

Not today. Not yet. He wasn't ready yet. But one day, perhaps quite soon, he would.